EGYPTIAN ADVENTURES

EGYPTIAN ADVENTURES

Olivia E. Coolidge

HOUGHTON MIFFLIN COMPANY BOSTON

The Riverside Press Cambridge

Illustrated by Joseph Low

TABLE OF CONTENTS

INTRODUCTION

AS OUR KNOWLEDGE of Egyptian history depends on the paintings, writings and monuments which the Egyptians left behind them, it follows that we know best the periods in which the country was prosperous. When Egypt was torn by civil wars or plundered by foreign invaders, its people spent their energies in a struggle to survive, and they had no time to interest themselves in cultural matters. For this reason, about three thousand years of Egyptian history is represented to us by the monuments of three great periods known as the Old, the Middle, and the New Kingdoms. The Old Kingdom has left us the pyramids, the Middle Kingdom much art and some literature, and the New Kingdom all kinds of records, varying between diplomatic correspondence with foreign kings to remains of houses or pictures of everyday life. It is this third period, dating from about 1600 B.C. to 1100 B.C., which is the subject of these stories.

The New Kingdom was the age in which Egyptian life was at its most colorful and varied. Great men had become fabulously rich, but little men were as miserably poor as ever. Merchants and soldiers learned foreign ways by traveling widely. Even people who stayed at home rubbed shoulders with hundreds of thousands of foreign-born traders, soldiers, and slaves. A fierce conflict developed as the old customs of Egypt fought against the introduction of new ideas. Both luxury and confusion sprang from foreign conquest. The most important thing about the New Kingdom was that it was an age of empire.

Thothmes III was the great soldier and statesman who conquered Syria and brought to Egypt immense plunder in the form of slaves and foreign treasures. The riches of the empire paved the way for Egypt's golden age, and yet the new influences produced a conflict that in a few generations pulled Egypt's greatness down.

Akhenaton, great-great-grandson of Thothmes, was the religious genius who brought chaos to Egypt by trying to substitute the worship of a single god for that of many. Lofty as were Akhenaton's ideas, he was himself an impractical dreamer who was so busy building a city for his new religion that he paid no attention to the frantic appeals of his representatives in Syria. By the time Akhenaton died, Syria was almost completely overrun by enemies, and the whole of Egypt seemed on the verge of revolution.

In the reign of Tut-ankh-amon, a son-in-law and successor of Akhenaton, the new religion of Aton was completely abandoned. Akhenaton's city was hastily deserted, and he himself became a "nameless Pharaoh" whom people were forbidden to mention. Tut-ankh-amon died before he was twenty, but by some miracle his tomb with its golden shrine and rich furniture escaped destruction, and it is Tut-ankh-amon whose name recalls to us most vividly the glory of the Egyptian past.

After the time of Akhenaton, the Egyptian empire only partially regained its power. The most successful attempt to restore it was made by Rameses II, about whom we know a great deal because he blew his own trumpet so extremely loud. One of his favorite tricks was to have his name cut on the bases of statues which had really been put up many years before in honor of earlier Pharaohs. Rameses' long reign was the last prosperous period of the New Kingdom. Decay had set in, and even before his death the power and wealth of Egypt had begun to crumble away.

The coming of the Israelites to Egypt probably took place during a period of foreign invasion before the New Kingdom arose. The Exodus under Moses seems to have occurred in the reign of the successor of Rameses and to be in itself a symptom of how greatly Egyptian power was falling away. Of the influence of the Israelites on Egypt during these four hundred years, we know nothing. We can only say that the ideas of Akhenaton were not in themselves Egyptian, but were characteristic of the Eastern peoples to which the Israelites belonged.

The stories in this book are each inspired by some thing which the Egyptians have left us: a picture of men hunting, an appeal for help to Pharaoh, or a fragment of a story about an enchantress who lived by a ford. They show us people of all classes and ages — some rich, some poor; some happy, some not. Perhaps because their religion was so hard and formal, there was a strange streak of harshness in Egyptian lives. People accepted sorrow and pain as a part of living, and they did not waste much pity on suffering. Instead, they all enjoyed to the full what they had: the gorgeous festivals, the blue lotus flowers, and the busy tempo of life along their mighty river. In the next world, they could imagine nothing better than more of the pleasures of this one over again. There was nothing dull about life to the Egyptians. These stories, which might have been told or might have happened, give a picture of a people who were intensely alive. It is this quality that makes them exciting to read about, even though their civilization has long gone by.

EGYPTIAN ADVENTURES

THE FEAST OF CATS

IT WAS STILL DARK in the shadows of the date palms and under the thick mud walls of the houses, but as Asenath and Bata emerged onto the raised road leading down to the river, they could perceive that dawn was at hand. By the time that Bata had taken off his clothes to plunge into the marshes for blue lotus flowers, the lazy quacking of half-awakened ducks was audible near the group of shelters that huddled around the landing place.

It was cold for Asenath in her single thin garment as she caught the wet flowers Bata threw to her. She was shivering before he had rinsed off the mud and put on his clothes again. His best kilt, washed months ago when the river water ran clearest, was as white as a rich man's, even if a little coarser. Today he was wearing an upper garment twisted together over his chest and leaving free his brown arms, now glistening with water. A blue headcloth, a trifle faded, was drawn smoothly across his forehead and hung down on either side of his face, covering his hair.

"We must hurry to the landing," Bata said as he settled

the skin of beer over his shoulder. "We have to make our garlands before the sun comes up."

Several people were already busy by the boat when Asenath and Bata reached the riverside. It was the market boat for the village, fairly big, but battered and dirty, even though for days the men had been trying to scrub her out. A new coat of paint could not be afforded, and the patched brown sail would have to do. However, on the high peaked prow stood a blue cat carved out of wood which had eyes of a glistening green stone with pupils of silver. Some daring souls had once stolen this from the prow of a rich man's boat at the festival. Since then the village had defended the blue cat against the envy of every settlement on the river as far down as the City of Cats.

Asenath had tucked a lotus into her hair, and her hands were busy weaving garlands out of the flowers that were heaped on the landing by each new group as it came. The men hung the garlands over the sides of the rickety cabin on the deck and festooned the prow. Before the sun rose they had finished, and the women declared the boat prettier than last year.

All now scrambled on board, disposing themselves on the rowing benches or the deck, and even climbing onto the roof of the unsteady little cabin to dangle their legs over the edge. One man took his stand by the great pole that ran through the stern to carry the rudder. Bata, with a lighter pole, watched by the prow for eddies and sandbanks. Two more men gave a good push from the bank before leaping on board. Over the eastern desert the rim of the sun came into view. They were off.

The boat swept along in fine style as the rowers put

their backs into their work and swung her into the current. All down the riverbank other boats were putting out, cheered on by hordes of little boys who danced on the landings, calling insults at the *Blue Cat* as she passed.

Another boat that had seen better days came poling cautiously out of an irrigation canal to the accompaniment of whistling and yelling. The battered head of a crocodile with half the lower jaw missing reared itself from her prow, and traces of former splendor could be seen in the pillars of faded red which propped up the corners of her cabin. The crew of the *Blue Cat* burst into shouts as they came alongside, while the women swung their rattles made of loose beads strung on parallel wires. Asenath felt the cabin shake as one of the women on top leaped to her feet to gesture at the *Crocodile*.

"Don't you even mend your old tub to visit the goddess?" she screamed through the din.

A girl with a red necklace began a dance on the roof of the *Crocodile*, kicking up her legs in a professional fashion and bending her body so far back that at times her hands were almost on the ground. A tall, lean man standing with his pole at the bow turned to shout at the two helmsmen, who were so deafened by the whistles and the clashing of cymbals that they paid no heed. The lean man jabbed desperately at a swirl in the water, swinging the *Crocodile* away from it across the bow of the *Blue Cat*. Bata, leaping to the rail, thrust his pole at the oncoming boat and pushed furiously. There was a moment of struggling and shouting as the oars of the rowers interlocked. The *Crocodile* swayed slowly outward and crashed onto the sandbank the lean poleman had been trying to avoid. The dancer sat down with a bump on the roof, and the *Blue Cat*'s crew burst into derisive cheering. The lean man on the *Crocodile* lifted his arm and threw his pole at Bata with all his might.

The crew of the *Blue Cat* ducked hastily, and a sudden silence fell as the pole crashed against the cabin and fell clattering to the deck.

"You — Bata!" screamed the *Crocodile*'s poleman.

The *Blue Cat* burst out into cheers and yells, and those on the roof struck up a song. Asenath went over to Bata, who still stood by the prow.

"That fellow threatened you," she said in his ear. Bata laughed.

"Those Crocodiles!" he said, putting an arm around her. "Don't worry! We know about them. We had a fight with them last year."

The river was beginning to fill up with boats going down to the festival. The *Blue Cat* was overtaken by a gay little barge brightly painted and picked out with gilding. Under a light awning supported by pillars sat two rich men, feet close together and hands on their laps. They wore elaborate wigs with stiff rows of curls, and their wide collars were brilliant with gold and enamel. Beyond the barge was a fat old trading vessel with black-bearded Syrians on deck and Nubian slaves handling the poles. Another village boat was drifting downstream while the rowers changed over and the crew refreshed itself from a skin of beer.

"I never knew there were so many boats on the river," said Asenath after vainly trying to count the little fishing craft of tarred reeds which were swarming out of the marshes and from the irrigation canals.

Bata lay stretched on the deck beside her, cooling off in the shade. He jumped up to wave a mocking hand at the *Crocodile*, which was appearing around a bend about a quarter of a mile back. "Wait till we get down to Per-Bastet," he said to Asenath over his shoulder. "This is not even a tenth of the boats you will see when we arrive."

Per-Bastet was black with boats, blue with lotus garlands, and white with people. Long before the river had parted to run around the sacred island that lay in the middle of the town, the *Blue Cat*'s crew was edging slowly through crowds of boats looking for a landing. Crews were standing up, clashing cymbals, singing, and yelling. Big boats were pushing smaller ones aside. Fishermen were fighting with poles for a place at the bank, so that now and then someone or other splashed headlong into the stream.

The *Blue Cat* finally nosed into the bank by the meadows above the town, and its crew plunged ashore into a scene of still wilder confusion.

"Lucky Charms!"

"Figs and melons!" yelled the hucksters.

"Offerings for the sacred cats!"

"Spare a poor blind man an offering for the festival!"

"See the magician change sticks into serpents! The marvel of the age!"

Asenath turned out of curiosity, but Bata pulled her past. "If we give what we have to the magician," he reminded her sternly, "how can we spend at the temple as we have planned? In the first month of our marriage, it is well to buy a blessing."

"Mats!" yelled the voices. "Mats to make shelters against the cold!"

"These can wait until the evening," said Bata. "If we leave them here, they will be stolen, and we cannot carry them all day. Come on to the city, so that we may offer our gifts while they are fresh."

"Wait!" Asenath grasped him by the elbow. "Let these two go by." She pointed at the man from the *Crocodile* and the dancing girl with red beads, who were pushing through the outskirts of the crowd around the magician.

"They don't matter," said Bata confidently. "Come on!"

For the rest of her life Asenath found cats a symbol of Per-Bastet and of everything that she and Bata did or saw at the festival there. Yellow cats brought back a memory of the wide avenue leading downward to the river, of the tree-shaded temple on the island, like a bright coin in the center of a bowl. Brindled cats with torn ears represented the narrow alleys where the flimsy shacks of the poor huddled together, and where life went on around open drains in the middle of the street. White cats haunted the temple gateway with its flagpoles and the shady forecourts, where the crowd shouted and bargained with hucksters. Cats swarmed purring around the long tables of offerings, rubbing themselves against the legs of the hairless priests.

It was cheaper to bring presents than to buy them. Bata unwrapped six fish caught in the Nile and kept fresh in wet green leaves during the journey down. Asenath had baked cakes, a little plain to be sure, since she had no colored sugar to ornament them. Still, she had shaped them like fish, mice, and cats for the pleasure of the goddess, who would appreciate the skill of a housewife, even where the ingredients were few.

Bata drew her over to a corner and began haggling with a vendor for a figure of the cat-headed goddess, brightly painted and fitted with a hole in the top through which the man obligingly ran a small string.

"Put it round the bride's neck," he said encouragingly to Bata, winking one of his red-rimmed eyes in a knowing fashion. "Seven sons will the figure of Bast bring to the pretty one if I have any skill with signs. Your copper back in ten years, pretty lady, and a good silver ring in addition if you cannot come into the temple with seven fine sons by your side."

"Perhaps — " began Asenath, smiling, but the seller of charms had already lost interest in her.

"Lucky figures! Blessings to the bride! This way, pretty lady!" He darted out into the courtyard to seize a young pair hurrying by.

"Save your breath for the seven sons," advised Bata, laughing as he urged Asenath toward the columned halls of the temple itself.

Here too were cats of white, ocher, or black, in the paintings that glowed on the dim walls in rich contrast to the glaring sunlight without. Here Pharaoh, in his golden headdress with the hooded snake on his forehead, was to be seen presenting offerings or being blessed. Behind him stood his wife and attendants, painted smaller out of respect for his greatness. The goddess Bast, on a golden throne, received his sacrifice, her cat head drawn in profile, and her body clad in a single tight garment like that which Asenath wore. Elsewhere Bast appeared again with other gods, hawk-headed and jackal-headed, regarding Pharaoh as he busied himself with his various activities on earth.

Asenath and Bata marveled at the vast columns of the temple, gazing with awe at the huge stone capitals picked out with red and blue. They puzzled over the painted inscriptions on the walls, in which words were represented by pictures of eyes, arms, birds, and other symbols, so beautifully executed that the writing was a pleasure even to those who could not read.

"The shrine of the goddess is closed today," said Bata. "Tomorrow when the image comes out, there will be a great procession."

In all the courts of the city as the sun grew low, fires began to glow in the roasting pits, and two or three fat geese at a time twirled on the spits, dropping sizzling grease on the embers. For a small copper ring, the cooks would carve you a leg, or a wing and a great fat slice of breast, and would give you a deep draught of beer from the jar that stood ready beside them. All along the walls of the rich men's gardens blazed lamps with little wicks floating in oil. The wide avenue leading down to the temple was lighted in this way from end to end. People were calling their wares along it, while men and women were dancing to the sound of pipes.

All the cats seemed black at night in Per-Bastet. Later still, when Asenath lay by her husband in a small reed shelter out on the meadow, the cats were only howling voices in the distance, no longer any color at all.

The second day of the feast started slowly. Everyone was tired with past pleasures and was in a mood for something new. All the Blue Cats had to meet in their corner of the meadow, exchange experiences, or display purchases. As they agreed, there was no need to hasten back to the city before the goddess came forth from her shrine.

"Be careful about the *Crocodile* fellow, Bata," added one of the men, getting up to go down to the river and plunge his head into the stream. "He was roaring up and down the avenue last night, as drunk as could be, looking for you. He has not forgotten how you made him give up the booty he stole from our shelter last year."

"He'll have a headache this morning," laughed Bata, "and leave me alone."

On this second day of the festival, the great avenue was jammed with people as the goddess Bast moved out of her temple to bestow her yearly blessing on the earth. Before her went trumpeters and hosts of temple musicians with rattles and castanets. After these a crowd of devotees came tumbling and howling, beating each other with clubs until blood flowed, though not much considering the noise that they made. Negro dwarfs and dancing jesters capered behind them, followed by priestesses, flute players, fanbearers, and finally the boat of the goddess herself.

The image of Bast moved about her city in a cedarwood boat borne on the shoulders of priests. On it was a cabin with silver pillars in which Bast sat, protected by very fine curtains from the sun and the breath of the mob. White cats on the deck before and behind her were chained with bright ribbons fastened to collars of silver and looked out over the heads of the multitude with half-closed, arrogant eyes.

The populace set up a roar at the sight of the goddess and surged forward, lifting their arms and leaping in frenzied applause. The temple guards walking with the procession began to push and struggle to keep clear a path.

Bata felt a fierce blow on his back and staggered forward, hearing Asenath scream over the din. He crashed full into a guard, who swayed backward into the bearers so that the whole boat rocked, and for a moment it seemed as though the image would be upset. The cats leaped to their feet, and one, tearing loose from the ribbon that held her, jumped down into the midst of the crowd.

The people nearest the goddess screamed, and with good

reason, for the temple guards had clubs and began to use them, yelling to the multitude to fall back. The commotion, however, impelled those behind to press forward, so that here and there a woman fell and was trampled, while the horses of the charioteers behind the goddess began to plunge.

Bata fought his way through the crowd, his headcloth wrenched off after a nasty crack on his forehead from one of the guards. "Asenath," he yelled, struggling wildly. "Asenath!" But Asenath was not to be found.

Asenath had screamed as Bata staggered forward, and she cried out again when the crowd began to push and sway. "This way," said a voice in her ear as the mass of people yielded slightly behind her, and she felt herself jerked violently backward against the chest of the *Crocodile* man.

"Little fool!" he said roughly in her ear as she resisted. "Do you want to be trampled?" Indeed, at that moment Asenath lost her footing and only saved herself by clutching at his elbow. "This way," he commanded again, driving a furious fist into the stomach of a fat man pushing behind him. They struggled a few steps farther. Asenath's breath was coming in gasps, and she swayed as the crowd swayed, unable so much as to lift up an arm.

"Bata?" she cried the moment she found her mouth close to the lean man's ear.

"Over there!" he yelled nodding. "Catch him when he gets out." He began to work with fists and elbows, and Asenath tried to follow him.

They came out on the edge of the crowd, disheveled and panting. "Over there!" said the lean man again, pointing to a swirl in the crowd. He took Asenath by the wrist and began to hurry her down the street, keeping close to the walls, where the struggling crowd had thinned out.

"Where is Bata?" cried Asenath, resisting furiously. The *Crocodile* man stopped by the mouth of an alley, where there was some slight breathing space.

"See him?" he inquired, pointing. Asenath turned away to look. With a fierce jerk the tall man pulled her into the alley and hustled her off down the street.

In the dirtiest little lanes of the poor quarter, the shacks lay huddled so closely that a man might easily touch both sides of a street at once with his hands. The naked children who played in the dust here took no notice of Asenath, and the blear-eyed old people in the doorways had learned long ago to mind their own business if anyone screamed. Except for the children and old folk, the quarter was empty, every man and woman being out on the streets during festival time, when stealing was brisk.

The lean man turned into the courtyard of what had perhaps once been an inn, but was now little more than a heap of tumbledown bricks. On one side a doorway gaped, and a roasting pit, blackened and smoking, showed that people not only lived here but on feast days had something to cook.

"In there," he said, setting Asenath down and giving her a push. "Sit down and stop yelling." He slapped her in the face as she opened her mouth, and drove her into a corner where a few old mats, somebody's bedding, were strewn on the earthen floor.

"That is enough to keep her quiet for a while," protested the girl with the red beads, getting up from the corner to give Asenath room. "What do you want to do with the girl?"

"There's a trader I know in town for the festival," answered he, straightening up and panting, "who'll sell her upriver in Thebes, and no questions asked. I owe that much to Bata on account of last year."

The girl bent down to take Asenath's hands away from her face as if to examine her. In doing so, she turned her back on the lean man for an instant. "Wait!" she indicated silently with her lips to Asenath, whose terrified eyes were staring at her wildly. "Wait!"

Asenath answered with a gulp that was almost a gasp, and the girl straightened up hurriedly before the lean man could become too curious. "Pretty enough," she pronounced aloud. "Have you talked to this trader?"

"I saw my chance and I took her," complained the lean man, dabbing at his face. "Do you think I foresaw this? I know where this fellow sleeps in the town, and I'll find him before morning."

"Go fetch some water and wash off your face where she scratched it," said the girl impatiently. "Before morning? And my uncle, whose house you have borrowed for this traffic of yours, will he stay out all night?"

The man picked up a jar. "I'll find the trader this afternoon somehow," he promised carelessly. "She cannot be moved until it is dark." He lounged away.

"Quick!" said the girl, turning sharply to Asenath. "Do you have any token I can send to the crew of the *Blue Cat*? Stop crying and answer."

"Let me go!"

The girl laughed contemptuously. "In broad daylight through the thieves' quarter? You would not get past three doors. This figure of Bast around your neck — do they know it? Where will they be?"

"In the meadow where the ropewalkers and the tumblers are to perform."

"Good. Lie still and be silent, as you value your life."

"What are you doing?" demanded the lean man, stooping to re-enter the door.

"She was begging me to let her go," drawled the girl casually. "Tie her up while I go to my cousin's for some food to pass the time until dark."

The longest afternoon of Asenath's life wore away slowly to the sound of distant music and the cries of children outside in the street. Once or twice she heard footsteps and a mumble of speech in the courtyard. Her heart bounded with hope, and dropped back with a sickening bump as no one came. Twice the girl entered with water, and Asenath drank greedily, for the heat in the little cabin was stifling as the sun poured down on the roof.

"Did you find the Blue Cats?" she said eagerly, but the girl only gestured for silence with an anxious look at the door.

At last when it was dark in the cabin, and objects seen through the doorway had melted into a shapeless gray blur, the dancing girl came in for the third time and busied herself for a moment in another corner of the room. Presently a small wick stuck in a dish of suet began to burn with a pale, evil-smelling flame. The girl brought it over to Asenath's side and began sawing at her bonds with a knife.

"I sent your token to the *Blue Cat's* men," she said in a hasty whisper, putting her mouth close to Asenath's ear. "But I dared not tell them to come to this quarter or betray my uncle's house. They are to meet us after dark where the great avenue runs by the Nile. Can you walk?"

Asenath tried to stand up, but fell back. With an impatient sound the girl put down her lamp again and bent to massage the blood back into Asenath's feet. Asenath leaned forward to help her, and the heads of the two nearly met.

"What is the matter?" asked the dancing girl sharply.

"My feet hurt," said Asenath feebly, and she bent forward again.

She could not be mistaken in the lamplight. The dancing girl had a string around her neck under the red beads, the very same string that the red-eyed vendor had threaded through the image of Bast. Asenath could even see the outline of the little figure thrust into the top of the dancing girl's dress.

"Water!" she muttered to gain time.

If no token had gone down to the *Blue Cat*, then no one would be waiting on the avenue by the edge of the Nile. Could the dancing girl merely have thought it easier to lead Asenath down to the river by the hand than to carry her swathed up like a mummy and bundled in old reed mats? On a festival night men did not carry burdens, and any party of jolly souls might interfere with such work being done. Asenath drank slowly, but her mind was racing.

"She will grip me tight by the wrist," she decided, "if she plans to betray me. If not, she would surely say, 'Hold onto me.' "

A strong grip fastened on her wrist as the thought went through her mind. "Come on!" said the dancing girl, blowing out the lamp before rising. "In case we need it, I have a knife in my other hand."

The narrow alleyway was perfectly dark, save that a few doorways were lighted by a feeble flame from inside. The dancing girl slid very quietly past these, pressing close against the opposite wall. Asenath followed obediently, straining her ears, for it had occurred to her with a sudden shock that the man must be near them to see that all went well. She heard nothing at all, but one time, glancing behind her, she saw a dark shape steal past one of the doorways. She gasped softly with sickening fear, and the girl jerked impatiently at her arm.

Her best plan was to dart down a cross street, but these came unexpectedly in the darkness and were always accompanied by a tightening of the grip on her wrist. She felt desperately along the walls for a weapon, but her hand lighted on nothing more satisfactory than a rotten rope hanging loose from the thatch.

The music and the shouting were louder now, and lights flickered in the distance. They avoided two men coming noisily homeward by ducking into a side street until they had passed.

Now or never, thought Asenath desperately, thinking of the knife.

The men lumbered past, and the dancing girl darted out again into the roadway, in a hurry perhaps to keep her distance from the following man. There was a fierce miauling as something moved under her feet. She tripped. On the instant, Asenath wrenched herself free and fled desperately into the dark.

She had the wit to turn away from the lights and music, and to pause and listen before she was too much out of breath. In a small shack beside her, someone was snoring. Asenath crept in through the door and held her breath as she heard feet approach. They halted outside and people muttered. The voice of the lean man rose in angry protest.

By Asenath's side, the sleeper turned over and raised himself on his elbow to shout a complaint, while she stood like a stone.

Long after the footsteps outside had moved on, the man beside her kept drowsily muttering, seeming just as likely to wake up as to sink back to sleep. Asenath had to hold her breath back and let it out slowly, trying not to quiver with the desperate pounding of her heart. When at last the snoring recommenced, she had to listen through it for the slightest sound of movement in the street outside. Inch by inch she crept into the doorway and put a cautious foot into the street.

People were beginning to come home, and she was forced to make countless confusing detours to avoid them. Once she was fairly trapped between two groups and darted into a courtyard. Inside, as soon as she put a hand on the brickwork, she knew where she was. There was a light in the cabin where she had lain that afternoon, and she could hear someone moving. She crouched down beside a pile of rubbish, praying that if anybody looked out, her white dress would not betray her in the dark.

A low mutter testified that one of the groups in the alley had reached the wall. To her horror, the people stopped full in the gateway. In another moment they might be coming in.

It was too late to move from the rubbish heap, which afforded concealment from a casual glance out from the cabin but none from the gate. "There she is!" cried the triumphant voice of the dancing girl from the gateway. Asenath screamed.

There was a loud shout from the alleyway and a stumbling of men in a hurry. Asenath cried out again with all her

might, kicked at the lean man as he caught her, and struck
out at his face. "Asenath! Asenath!" called a voice outside.

"In here! In here!" she screamed with desperation.

There was a fierce rush through the gateway. Asenath,
receiving a last box on the ear from the lean man, staggered
and fell. Someone tripped over her, came down across her,
recovered, and hurled himself into the fray. The dancing
girl in her turn began to shout. More people rushed in
through the gateway, some of them armed with bludgeons,
and others with knives.

"Blue Cats this way!" cried Bata's voice beside her. "Can
you walk, Asenath? We shall have to be as quick as we
can." He put an arm around Asenath's waist and lifted her,
beginning to move toward the gateway as the Blue Cats fell
in alongside. "Now, all together!" he cried as they rushed
for the gateway. In another moment Asenath found herself half pushed, half carried down the alley, with the music
and the lights growing clearer ahead of her and the threatening shouts of her pursuers closer behind.

As long as there was fighting with the rear guard,
Asenath's strength sufficed to keep her on her feet. When,

however, they approached the lighted avenue, the shouts behind them died as the lean man and his friends thought it more prudent to desist. Suddenly Asenath was shaking with sobs and could do nothing but cling to Bata in a storm of crying. Stopping, he lifted her in both his arms and bore her into the light.

"How did you find me?" she asked Bata at last, as they laid her in the cabin of the *Blue Cat*, while the men quietly unshipped the oars and the women took down the faded garlands. "Someone saw you with that devil in the crowd," said Bata, "and we knew that he had friends in the thieves' quarter from the time when we fought him last year."

"If that girl had not tripped on a cat," said Asenath, clinging to him tightly, "I should have been gone from the courtyard long before you came."

"It was Bast who saved you," said Bata comfortingly. "Her protection is powerful for brides, and she remembered our offering. You shall yet bring your seven sons to make her a sacrifice."

"Not to Per-Bastet," said Asenath, trembling. "I have seen enough of the City of Cats."

THE CARPENTER'S DAUGHTER

THE MIDDAY MEAL was being served in Senmen's cookshop, and a glorious smell of boiling stew was drifting down the street. Careful people were hurrying home with their portions of hot meat, or even of gravy, saving themselves the price of fuel without buying a whole meal. Hungry barbers were flashirʒ their razors under people's noses and begging to shave them right in the cookshop for the price of their table scraps. Waiters were placing stools for customers under the awning and as far out into the street as there was any shade. In the back of the shop enormous pans were bubbling, ducks were roasting on spits, and servants were carrying fruits, coarse wine, and bread from an inner room.

Senmen himself was a round, greasy little man in a limp linen garment and a plain wig, from beneath which trickles of sweat would begin to appear at this time of day. He carried a staff for dignity's sake, but he generally employed it in poking the servants, whacking at thievish dogs, or shaking at beggars. Every familiar customer got a hearty word of welcome, while Senmen, who kept no scribe and did all his accounts in his head, rapidly calculated the present state of his client's credit. Strangers were bowed in with a flourish

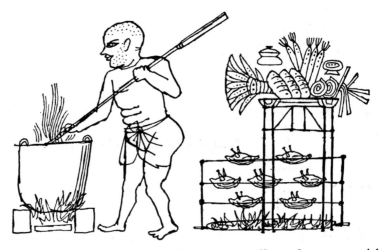

and after preliminary bargaining were allowed to pay with a fan or a new pair of sandals for a specified amount of roast duck, fruit, and honey cakes, washed down with vinegary wine.

As the meal hour wore on, the cookshop became hotter and smellier from the combination of the midday heat and the boiling stew. Senmen passed his hand over his face more often, while some of the customers, deciding to have their siesta where they were, slid off their stools and arranged themselves comfortably along the wall. Presently servants began to linger around the latecomers, and actually hustled away one unlucky barber before he could touch the remains that his customer had promised. Senmen liked to have a late meal with his particular cronies and generally managed to clear the shop of diners in excellent time.

"Don't make him a goldsmith," a wrinkled, dark-skinned man was saying in decided tones as the cookshop proprietor pulled up a stool and began to devour a half-cold portion of his stew. "There used to be a good living in our trade until the rich men bought their own artisans to make their jewelry. Nowadays we spend half our time in the street looking for business, and when we get any, it is the crudest work and miserably paid."

"Change trades with me if you like," retorted a dyer, holding up his wrinkled hands, stained an indelible purple color and smelling horribly of rotten fish. "At least people don't turn the other way when you come past."

"Nor do you work day and night to keep from starving," chimed in a shoemaker. "I declare that I have pulled so many straps tight with my teeth that even Senmen's stew tastes of badly cured leather."

"Well, don't suppose I find it particularly attractive my-self," retorted Senmen, "after serving it for hours in the boiling heat."

"Make him a scribe," said the elderly little goldsmith, sticking firmly to his original theme. "It is a huge sacrifice to keep him more than ten years in school, where he will earn nothing and eat enormously. Still, think of the results! I had an uncle who was keeper of one of the big temple granaries and lived like a rich man, and all because he learned how to read and write."

"Not much of an uncle, though," declared a man with red-rimmed eyes and heavily calloused hands who was a stonemason, and to whom the goldsmith's advice had been addressed. "He might have sent you to school and made you a scribe too, as it seems to me."

"He would have," asserted the goldsmith with a twinkle, "if it had not just then been discovered that he had stolen eight thousand bushels of wheat from the granary and sold them. But for this sad misfortune, I too should have become a great man."

"My sister's son is a scribe," commented Senmen, pushing aside his table with the remains of the loathsome stew. "He keeps the accounts of a master carpenter and was to marry my daughter. Strangely enough, in spite of his excellent prospects, she will not look at him."

"Toui will not look at him?" cried the shoemaker, raising his long, lean hands in shocked surprise. "Your own sister's son, and actually a scribe?"

"Beat her," suggested the stonemason laconically.

"I did," replied Senmen, "and she poured some horrible mixture into my beer which spoiled it all. It is cheaper to leave her alone."

"I wondered why we were drinking this wine," commented the dyer, shaking his head over its miserable quality. "Young people have no respect for their elders any more."

"Toui has some other lover," declared the shoemaker positively, "or she would not be such a silly girl."

"She has as many as there are flies in my cookshop," cried Senmen, dislodging a buzzing swarm from the remains of food on his table to illustrate his point. "All the riffraff in the district is crawling about my yard. It is high time she was settled with Tinro, who is perfectly steady and never looks at any other girl."

"That is undoubtedly the trouble," remarked the goldsmith sagely. "Get him to pay some attention to the carpenter's daughter for a change."

"The carpenter hasn't one," retorted Senmen gloomily, "and in any case, Tinro is not at all that kind of young man."

"Well then, he needs a helping hand, and we'll invent a girl for him," said the goldsmith laughing. "It would be hard if my own five daughters had not taught me how to manage such things. Will you pay me a month's free meals,

Senmen, if I show you how to make your Toui change her mind?"

"Potluck, then," said Senmen, calculating values.

"In that case I must have beer with the meal, and not this wine."

"How much beer?"

"Look here," cried the goldsmith impatiently, "do you want Toui settled, or don't you? Is it a bet?"

"A bet!" exclaimed the shoemaker vigorously, bringing down the flat of his hand on his table. "We three will play umpire and see that the goldsmith has a fair chance."

The house of Senmen was built over and behind his shop, looking out on to a courtyard that had once belonged to a single house but was now common ground for several families. Behind the cookshop itself lay the bakery and storeroom, from which a passage led to the ground-floor sleeping rooms. During the day it was cooler upstairs, where a breeze was brought down by funnels from the roof, and where wide shaded balconies gave light through doorways to the almost windowless rooms. Here after the siesta Senmen found his daughter pressing linen garments into folds, which she produced by dampening the starched material and smoothing it with her hand over corrugated boards. He noted with annoyance that the clothes were but half done, though she had found time to tint her lips, paint blue shadows around her large, liquid eyes, and attend to the elaborate dressing of her hair. Furthermore, the pastry cook's son from next door was below in the courtyard, instead of preparing almond paste as he should be doing for tomorrow's cakes. He was an unattractive, pimply fellow, who was known to be far too often at the beer shop. Senmen felt there was no accounting for young women's tastes.

Aroused by these disturbing reflections, he strode out onto the balcony and began to expostulate with his daughter in ringing tones. "I told you that Tinro would tire of your flightiness," he cried, plucking off his wig and filling his palm with water to cool his shaven head. "Now he has written a wonderful poem to the carpenter's daughter, Tausert."

"She is welcome to it," declared Toui, giving her head a scornful toss that set dancing the countless little clay balls she had worked into the ends of her hair to make it stand out in masses around her face. "I hope for her sake that what Tinro writes is a little less dull than what he says to me."

"It is a beautiful love poem," retorted her father, conscious of interest from the opposite balcony where the pastry cook's plain and ill-natured daughters had pricked up their ears. "As for what it says about you, I must admit that you have deserved every word by your flirtatious ways."

"How dare Tinro mention my name?" cried Toui, stamping. "I will never speak to him again as long as I live."

"I don't suppose you will ever have the chance," replied Senmen, slapping back his wig into place. "The carpenter's daughter is a better match, and pretty too."

With this last shot he withdrew and was able to report to his friends by the next afternoon that three different versions of Tinro's poem, all insulting, had been audibly recited in the courtyard, accompanied by titters. "Toui spoiled a whole batch of honey cakes in her fury," he added in complaining tones. "Really, the expense of this plan is too great to be born."

"The next stage will be even more costly," the goldsmith asserted, unmoved by this lamentation. "Surely you must know by this time that young girls are a terrible expense!"

Two or three days after this conversation, Senmen made his peace with his daughter by giving her a little bracelet which he had bought from the goldsmith after many protesting groans. "I got it cheaply because it is broken," he told her untruly, "but the goldsmith is enough in my debt to repair it if you take it to him."

Toui thanked him with a kiss and set out across the market square, not omitting to brighten the effect of her tight linen dress with a necklet of beads, two other bracelets, and a flower tucked into the fillet around her hair. Thus attired, she attracted a considerable number of admiring glances. She felt her spirits rising for the first time since they had been crushed by Tinro's unspeakable behavior. She looked from under her long lashes at a young man selling pots, and the young man smiled at her. She tossed her head at a handsome fellow in immaculate linen, and wriggled her shoulders as a fishmonger turned to admire her retreating back. By the time she entered the street of the goldsmiths, she looked very much like a honey pot that had sailed through the market, collecting a noisy train of attendant flies.

Toui was making a greater error than she knew, since the goldsmith, who had been waiting for her arrival since the siesta, might easily have missed it during an exciting argument over a poor old woman's beads. Warned by the noise of a too familiar whistle, he perceived her just in time to give up the battle and send out his slave to bring Tinro on to the scene.

"Tell him that Toui wants him to buy a bracelet, and make sure that he comes running immediately," he ordered.

Toui sailed briskly into the shop of the goldsmith and showed him her bracelet, while the more devoted of her admirers disposed themselves in lounging attitudes outside in the street. In a leisurely fashion the goldsmith set out his smallest hammer by the anvil, took up his pincers, and put his blowpipe to his lips to heat the flame. He was able to spin the job out to two or three operations, since as he observed, he could not toss the ornament into the crucible and melt it all down, but must heat and hammer out a very small piece at a time.

After the soldering, the gold must be cooled in water, cleaned carefully with sand, and polished up. "I do not know when I have seen a prettier bracelet," remarked the goldsmith, holding it to the light, breathing on it, and rubbing away at a dirty spot with his thumb. "Or a prettier girl to wear it," he added smiling.

Toui lifted her eyebrows a little, not that compliments ever surprised her, but that experience had made her suspicious. The goldsmith's second daughter had good cause to complain about Toui, whose conscience made her wonder uneasily where this conversation would end. Looking around for a change of subject, she started to fidget with some unfinished work by the anvil. "Is that just a plain bracelet which you are hammering there?" she inquired.

The goldsmith appeared equally happy to talk of this bracelet, which he described as the only good order he had lately received. Ten minutes passed while he got out the stones that were to be set in it and showed them to Toui, scratching diagrams in the dust on the floor to explain how they might be arranged. "It is a bridal gift," remarked he, sitting back on his heels and glancing out at the street, in which a young man in a violent hurry had finally appeared. "It is for a master carpenter's daughter from her bride-groom, a talented young scribe."

"How delightful!" said Toui in a strained voice, crimsoning with fury, but relieved to find that the goldsmith was no longer looking at her.

"Why, here is the scribe himself," he exclaimed with an air of surprise which was on the whole well affected, considering that he had been wondering whether Tinro would ever appear.

"Toui!" cried Tinro, stretching out both hands to her and delightedly beaming.

Toui looked at him speechlessly for a moment, while tears of indignation gathered in her beautiful eyes. "How dare you speak to me?" she cried at last, pushing hastily past him and fleeing up the street, pursued by the calls of her waiting admirers.

Tinro stared unhappily after her. He was a very tall, thin young man with knobbly knees and elbows who poked his head and frowned in a shortsighted way that gave him a worried expression. "How am I to marry her without ever speaking to her?" he objected. "I wish she would not treat me in this unreasonable way."

"She is shy of you, perhaps," suggested the goldsmith with kindly interest. Tinro pondered this idea in his slow fashion, and shook his head.

"No," he said decidedly, dismissing the notion. "Not Toui!"

"Well then, you should manage her better," retorted the goldsmith, "and a man with five daughters of his own is the very individual to teach you how to do so properly."

Tinro responded to his education so gratifyingly that the goldsmith was able to report the sale of the beautiful bracelet when next he dined with Senmen. "Tinro is not as stupid as he looks," he remarked with approval, "and he perfectly well understands when I tell him that actions speak louder than words. I think we might now have him jilt the carpenter's daughter, whom we will make exceedingly ill from chagrin."

"And what is this new move going to cost me?" asked Senmen with sour suspicion.

"A month's free meals," replied the goldsmith with confidence, "including beer."

He might have felt more dubious about this result, had he realized that Toui was at that moment painting red on her lips with the intention of going down to deal with the carpenter's daughter. Actually, it had never occurred to her not to marry Tinro, who was, as she perfectly well knew, an excellent match. She had, however, frequently wondered if anything would make him more dashing, and had even sighed slightly for the pastry cook's son, who was wicked enough to drink too much. She had never gone so far as to dream of such unheard-of, such outrageous behavior as breaking off a marriage arranged by her father and agreed on by the neighborhood at large. Toui was now angry that she had not thought of this expedient before Tinro had done so, but she was also perfectly aware that her position would be awkward if she did not get her lover back. Even the pastry cook's son was affianced to the gold-smith's second daughter, and, wicked as he was, he would never throw over his bride for a girl who had been jilted by somebody else. Mingled with all these new ideas in Toui's mind was an increased respect for Tinro. She never would have thought he had it in him to take such decided steps.

Absorbed in these reflections, Toui made her way through the market, rewarding her various admirers with a blank unseeing stare. As she turned into one of the narrow streets, she stepped into a recess to avoid a pair of asses laden with hay which were taking up the road. A shopkeeper lying in wait for customers darted out like a spider. Toui shook him indifferently off her arm, but the incident served to make her wonder how she could get into the carpenter's house. A young girl could not loiter in the Theban streets, even for a moment, without children, beggars, Negro porters, foreign soldiers, peddlers, shopkeepers, or even priests com-bining to hustle her or make her the target for rough jokes. Though perfectly used to this situation, and even enjoying it, Toui had no desire to be noticed in the carpenter's street.

Fortunately the carpenter's shop contained only two workmen, one planing a board with quick, skillful strokes of the adze, the other smoothing with pumice the roughly finished leg of a bed. Both stopped immediately at the sight of Toui and welcomed her in.

"I want to see Tausert, your master's daughter," said Toui. "Is she at home?"

The man with the pumice merely looked blank, but the one with the adze, who was younger, pushed forward a stool and gave his companion an elaborate wink. "Why not wait for a little?" he suggested, "She will have to come in through here to get into the house."

"Don't be a fool," said the older man impatiently. "Tell the girl she has come to the wrong shop and let her go."

"Unfortunately my father has no daughters," admitted the young man, "though I know how sorry he will feel about this when he sees you."

Crimson with embarrassment, Toui persisted, but the young man only became more positive as she tried to explain. "Tinro write poems!" exclaimed he. "I don't believe it! Neither would you if you had ever seen him yourself!"

"Don't be a fool," said the older man again. "Of course she has seen him. I rather think," he added, turning kindly to Toui, "that the young scribe has been inventing a girl to make you jealous."

Toui nodded with tears in her eyes. She was beyond speech, but she felt the conclusion was inescapable.

"You know," said the workman, "I rather like him for being so ingenious. It is really much easier to forgive than if he had flirted with somebody real. Now as far as we are concerned, you never came here, and you do not care about the carpenter's daughter in the least. I should marry Tinro, however, if I were you. He seems to have earned it."

"That's right," said the younger one. "But if you would like just a little revenge on him first, you might always call on me. It would be very pleasant." He winked at her.

"Thank you," said Toui, winking back and feeling better. "Perhaps it might be enjoyable sometime."

"The girl doesn't need any help to make that sort of trouble," commented the older man sourly as they watched Toui's retreating back. "She will not be an easy wife to handle, and I think the better of Tinro for the way he has dealt with her."

"Whoever would have thought," said the younger one reflectively, "that an earnest young fellow like Tinro had it in him to make up such a tale?"

This was rather the opinion of Toui when the first embarrassment of her discoveries in the carpenter's shop had worn away. She began to find herself looking forward to marriage, if not with excitement, at least with an interest in the possibilities of Tinro's character. She actually turned her face away from the pastry cook's son as they met in the courtyard, and she received the news that the carpenter's daughter had been jilted with a total lack of concern.

"I always expected it," she said to her father. "Nobody could be really fond of a girl like that."

Senmen was completely taken aback by this retort and afraid to continue the conversation, lest too much about the carpenter's daughter be revealed. However, he reported that things were going well and was encouraged a day or two later by Toui's acceptance of the bracelet, which Tinro did not bring in person, on the goldsmith's advice. He was of the opinion that Tinro was not to be trusted with the story of the carpenter's daughter because he was far too stupid to keep up the pretense.

"If she once gets a chance to speak to him, she will have the truth out of him in half a minute," said he.

"How are they ever to get married if they do not speak?" asked Senmen reasonably.

"They need a go-between for the present moment, and

later on they may meet each other in public for a while,"
said the goldsmith. "I will arrange it all." He bustled away.

Matters were at this agreeable stage for several days, during which the goldsmith boasted insufferably about his coming free meals and beer. The little club at the cookshop,
though horrified, was almost pleased when this complacent
mood was shattered by the news that Toui had eloped with
the pastry cook's young man. They discussed the matter in
muffled tones in a corner of the cookshop while Senmen
was busy serving a very late customer.

"I always said," commented the dyer, "that no good
would come of Toui's goings-on."

"He'll beat her," declared the stonemason, a man of one
idea.

"I dare say he will," replied the goldsmith, who seemed
strangely undismayed by his disappointment. "It will do
her all the good in the world, and she will see that he keeps
out of the beer shop. I consider it a most suitable match!"

"One might think that you had planned the whole thing,"
said the shoemaker disgustedly. "What happened to that
ingenious scheme of yours?"

"Well," admitted the goldsmith, "even a man with five
daughters cannot be right about girls every time. I made
the mistake of choosing my second daughter for a go-between because she is naturally sympathetic. Unfortunately,
she was engaged to the pastry cook's son and was jealous because she could not manage him. I am afraid that she must
have betrayed the entire plot to him in a fit of pique. Naturally Toui would not think of marrying Tinro, once she
heard that we had been laying bets on it."

"Naturally," agreed the shoemaker. "I must say it serves
you and your second daughter right."

"As a go-between," said the goldsmith smugly, "my daughter found Tinro needed a good deal of sympathy, I expect."

"You mean — " interrupted the dyer in astonished tones. The goldsmith nodded.

"It means the end of my free meals," he said regretfully. "But I have made a nice little profit, and after all Tinro is an excellent match."

THE LUCK CHARM

MOTHER WENT OUT before dawn on washday to get a good place on the river, but she was not too much hurried to remind me that I must look after the house.

"Those good-for-nothing neighbors have their eyes on my luck charm," she declared as she tore pieces off the hard dark loaf which served us for breakfast. "A lot of thieves they are, and let me tell you there is not a household in town with a charm as handsome as mine."

I promised faithfully to look after the luck charm.

"Right here in the house," insisted Mother. "No playing up and down the street."

"No, Mother."

Old Muti from next door began to bang so hard on the partition that little pieces of dry mud broke off it and cascaded to the floor.

"Just coming!" yelled Mother hastily, shouldering her bundle. "You keep your hands off that loaf while I am out. I know just how much food there is left." With this parting shot from the threshold, she marched firmly away.

Father and I groped for our bread in the dark, since lamp oil was precious. We sat cross-legged, chewing slowly,

while the faint gray light in the doorway grew gradually
stronger. Father gave me a sip of his beer, as he always did
when we were alone, but he was saving his breath for heaving on the long ropes hour after hour, and he did not speak.
As soon as we could see the outlines of the doors across the
street, he shuffled away, dragging his feet, as workmen do to
save lifting. I finished my breakfast alone.

The housework did not take long. I stirred up the rushes
which served us for beds, made a few scratch marks on the
dirt floor with a broom of twigs, and considered things tidy.
I inspected the grain bin thoughtfully and studied the mud
seal that fastened it. A handful of grain was something to
chew on and very likely would not be missed, but I should
get a terrible beating if Mother found the seal had been
disturbed.

The seal on the grain bin was hopeless. I gave it up and
sauntered to the doorway in order to glance into the street.
I was supposed to sweep the alley too, I remembered.
Mother had been brought up in a proper house with a yard
of its own and a sycamore tree to sit under. She never could
get used to the melon rinds and fish heads which other people tossed out, and which usually drifted up toward our
door because we lived at the end of the street, jammed right
up against the wall. I picked up a couple of rotten onions
and lobbed them experimentally down the road, aiming for
the fifth doorway, where I knew they only had girls who
were too small to interfere. Unfortunately, they landed by
Sety's, and he must have known it was our washday, because
he came tearing out to return the onions much faster than
they had come. One squashed full on my forehead as I
dodged back into the doorway, thankful I had not started
my cleaning up with anything hard.

After that it was no use trying to clear the roadway. Sety was at least two years older than I and almost big enough to go to work with his father, which I heartily wished he would do. "I'll teach you to throw your garbage down here," he was yelling. "I'll have half the fish heads in town in front of your door, and I dare you to move them." He knew perfectly well that Mother would whip me if she had to wade through a mess to get in.

There didn't seem much use in being good any longer when things had once started to go wrong. Our gang was already out in the street, and if it had not been for Sety, I should have joined them. All the children in town had a new game which we had been playing furiously for three or four days. You marked out the ground in squares with your toe and put down a piece of broken pot. Then you hopped on one foot from each square to the next one, kicking the potsherd as you went. It was a good game because we laid bets on it, and there was a chance of winning a rope, or a colored stone, or a bit of real copper wire. The night before, Father had brought me a treasure worth a really good wager — a broken bit of tile thrown out by the builders from Pharaoh's new palace, and painted with the picture of a duck's head as clear as could be.

I decided to go up to the roof, taking my duck's head for company, and see from there what our gang was doing. Later, if the coast was clear, I could go down and join in the game. On second thought, I went over to the earthen chest in which our best things were kept and got out the luck charm. Someone might come in while I was on the roof, and perhaps it would be safer with me.

Mother's luck charm was a flat, wide collar sewn with

tiny blue beads close together, from which a broad strip hung down the back, handsomely embroidered with holy signs in bright red. It had been handed down in Mother's family for a great many generations, and had always gone to the most beautiful child of the house. Mother, who had been one of eleven, had always expected great things from it someday, especially as it had brought her no good luck whatsoever.

Being a little boy still, I never wore clothes, except for a short kilt on feast days; so, having nowhere else to carry the luck charm, I put it on around my neck, hanging the red signs down between my shoulders where they would watch out for devils like eyes in the back of my head. When I was grown the charm would be mine, though, to be sure, there was not much glory in that for an only child.

By lying flat on my stomach with my head over the edge of the roof, I had a good view of the game going on in the street. Taia, standing on one leg in the second square, was wobbling a little as she looked at the potsherd, which lay just across the line of the third. This was a most difficult shot, as I very well knew, since Taia must now hop into the third square and kick into the fourth without landing with her foot on the line. Taia had her hand clutched round a bright reddish stone and was nearly in tears at the thought of losing it.

"Come on!" said several impatient people round the circle.

Taia bent forward to hop, but changed her mind and straightened up, wobbling more violently than before.

"Oh, give up, Taia!" yelled Pepy, stretching out his hand impetuously. Taia immediately put her foot down and burst out howling.

"It isn't fair! You pushed me," she whined.

"I did not," screamed Pepy indignantly. "Hand over the stone."

"He did not," I shouted, wriggling half off the roof to drop a centipede on Taia's neck. Pepy had always been a good friend of mine.

Taia gave a shriek and hurled her precious bit of stone at me with all her strength. Being only a girl, she missed completely, and in another minute Pepy had her by the hair and they were rolling over and over in the roadway. I paid her back with a bowlful of dirty water, but a good many other people got wet from that too, so that pretty soon all sorts of sticks and trash began to fly.

I judged it wise to make for cover, and took refuge in the space between our pavilion and the wall. The pavilion was a home-made wicker erection with three sides and a roof and faced in the direction of the prevailing wind. It was hotter than an oven on days like this when the air was still, but on stifling evenings when the heat rose up from the stinking alleyway, we could usually rely on catching a breath of cool, clean air up here. Beside it and partly shading it rose the wall, twice my height even here on the roof, stretching its unbroken length from end to end of our town. On the other side, I knew, lay the houses of overseers and stewards, and all the important men whom Pharaoh had put in charge of erecting his city, for which Father was hauling up stone from the barges on the Nile.

I took out my duck's head tile and used the sharp edge to scratch a crude sketch in the dried-mud wall of Taia screaming with a centipede draped over her neck. Presently a big piece of mud flaked off and spoiled the picture. The fact was, the town and the wall had been hastily put up to shelter the workmen. Both would be allowed to fall back into rubbish as soon as Pharaoh had completed the city he was building as a rival to Thebes. Indeed, it sometimes seemed as though there were a race between the permanent city that was rising and the temporary one that was trying to fall down. I found I could make quite a hole in the dried mud wall with my duck's head. If I could get a handhold of some sort, I might be able to look over the wall.

I began to work on a new hole a little higher up. It might be possible to climb up, since the wall was slightly tapered. The danger was that the mud would crumble further under my weight and let me down. It was hard work chipping with the broken tile held high above my head. Two or three times I had to lie down in the shade to cool off, but I kept at it, having nothing better to do with my time. I had started by scratching very carefully, but after a little while I got wilder, until finally I lifted back my arm and thumped at the wall with all my might.

Crack! An edge of my precious tile broke off and sang past my ear. I found to my dismay that my duck had no beak any more. I lost my temper, threw down the tile, and strolled across to the edge of the roof.

Below me the fighting seemed to be over, but the quarrel had passed into the stage of high-pitched yells of abuse. Sety was still hovering around, and I wished I had not stirred things up, or he might have lounged off to visit his favorite girl, who did not live on our street.

I went disconsolately back to the wall and picked at it sulkily, but almost immediately I laid my hand on it, I realized a whole brick had come loose. In another minute I had it out and my hand in the hole. Inside I felt the rough edge of a stone.

I started to caper for joy. Of course the bricks would be only a casing, inside which would be rubble and stones. It should be easy enough to get my hand around something solid while I put my foot in the lower hole and worked on another brick. I picked up the broken tile and started right away.

I had to make four more large holes before I got hold of the top of the wall, and over and over again I was forced to lie down in the shade, and even to fetch up some water to wash off the dust and the sweat. It was stifling up on the roof as the sun got higher, but perhaps that was just as well, since I had the place to myself. My breath was coming in gasps and my heart and head pounding as I finally got one hand up, then the other, and took a quick look over the wall.

Nothing was to be seen but some bushes and a pool. There was a house, but at a distance and half concealed by trees. With a fierce scramble I hoisted myself up and faced in to the street, the blood running down my scraped knees.

Below me the victorious party had gone back to their game. "Hey!" I called cautiously, lobbing a tiny stone to attract their attention. "Hey! Look at me!"

Pepy swung round immediately, and his eyes positively bulged. His jaw dropped as he put his hand up over his mouth. "Ooh!" he said. "How do you dare? If you're seen, they will *kill* you."

"Ooh!" chorused the rest of the admiring crowd.

I had never made such a sensation in my life, and the triumph of it went to my head. "Dare?" I retorted loftily. "You just look at me!"

I got to my feet, rather slowly because I seemed to be very high up and it was narrow at the top of the wall. I

began to dance and throw out my arms to show how well I
could balance, jumping higher and higher as I saw how
much my audience was impressed.

"Hey!" remarked a small voice distinctly from the other
side of the wall.

My heart gave a terrible flop, and I tried to turn round in
the middle of a leap to see who was below. Naturally I
came down off balance. I staggered, clutched at the coping,
lost my grip, and vanished from sight over the wall.

Mother's luck charm must have been very powerful to
bring me down on the top of a thick pile of rubbish that the
gardeners had left. Every bit of breath was shaken from
my body, but I did not even twist my arm or bruise myself
worse than I had often done by falling down the stairs.

"Hey!" said the small voice again from behind me as I

was trying to sort myself out. "Why did you jump off the
wall that way?"

I blinked and looked wildly around me. I found myself
lying in a small patch of ground backing up against the wall
and surrounded on the other three sides by masses of shrubs
covered with pinkish and purplish flowers. In a gap between
two of these stood a little girl so strange and beautiful that I
began making hasty signs in the air to protect myself in case
she might be a demon.

She was even smaller than I, but her skin was infinitely
finer and smoother. The nails of her feet and hands had
been lightly reddened, while someone had painted her lips
and used a delicate shadow around her large dark eyes. The
one long lock on her shaven head was not shaggy like mine,
but brushed and beautifully shining. She had no clothes,
but she was actually wearing rings and bracelets as grown-up
women do. About her neck there hung a collar so wide that
it covered her shoulders completely and hung down over
her breast, flashing in glittering rows of red, gold, blue, and
green. The edge of it was a border of blue lotus flowers, and
below it hung the sign of Aton, Pharaoh's new god, in the
shape of a great gold disc surrounded by rays, each ending
in a hand stretched out in blessing.

"W-what are you here for?" I stammered stupidly, meaning of course was she a demon of good luck or bad, but she
did not take it that way.

"I was just listening to those children on the other side of
the wall," she explained simply. "They were using all sorts
of words I never heard before in my whole life." She men-
tioned a few.

"Good gracious! You mustn't say those," I interrupted
hastily. "Whatever would your mother say?"

"I expect Mother would laugh," she said thoughtfully. "But then Nurse would be very angry indeed."

"Even *my* mother wouldn't let me say that," I remarked. "What do you want to listen to those bad children for?"

She sighed. "I wish I could play in the street without having grownups around."

I took a look at her immaculate hands and clear unbruised skin, and I shook my head slowly from side to side. "You wouldn't like it," I argued. "It's all melon rinds and stinking fish heads. You wouldn't like it at all."

"I never saw a real fish head," she persisted, "except alive of course. Does it smell any worse than these bushes? They make me sneeze."

"You wouldn't like it," I repeated doggedly, at a loss to explain how we lived. "Anyway you can't possibly climb over the wall."

"I know. We might play something here of course."

I considered this doubtfully, while I wondered how I was ever going to get home. A garden like this would certainly have a wall all around, and I dared not risk getting caught. "What can you play?" I temporized, feeling for the moment safer by the gardener's rubbish heap than anywhere else in the grounds.

"Well, there's this," said the little girl, diving into the bushes behind her and coming up with something in her arms. I went over to look. It was the figure of a child carved out of wood and beautifully painted, having a wig of real hair and a tiny dress with a red girdle. Its arms and legs were actually jointed so that it could sit down or stand up.

"I never saw anything like it except in a temple," I said with awe, putting out a finger to feel its soft, dark hair.

"Even the temple figures cannot sit down. What else will it do? Is it a god?"

"It won't do anything else," she answered, "but we could play that we were its mother and father and that under this bush was our house."

"I don't think that would be much fun," I said, uneasily conscious that her and my ideas of a house would not really agree. "I'll tell you what we'll do." Swiftly I drew a row of squares in the dust with my toe and looked around for a small piece of baked mud from the wall. "I'll show you just the same game that they're playing out in the street."

The little girl jumped up and down for joy, and I allowed her a few practice shots before I settled down to explain how the thing should be done. As I had suspected, she had never hopped on one leg in her life, let alone kicked a potsherd. It was hardly even worth winning from her.

"Let's play properly now," she said after a bit, "and lay bets like the others. If you win, you take my collar, and if I do, I must have yours."

I put my hand hastily up to the luck charm. "You can't take that. It's Mother's," I said.

"Of course I can have it," she retorted, stamping her foot. "After all, what else can you bet with?"

Well, that was true enough when I came to think of it, and in any case I did not suppose it possible that I should be beaten by a wretched girl who had never hopped before. All the same I took my time over my turn and went through all eight squares without a single fault before I turned the little piece of brick over to her.

She got into the second square by great good luck, and into the third by cheating a little, which I pretended I did not notice because she had her tongue out and was working

so terribly hard. When she put her foot down for the
second time, I thought I had better protest.

"You're out," I said. "You had both feet on the ground."

She turned on me angrily as though I ought not to have
spoken. "All right," she said, "but I ought to have had another chance because I'm practising. Still, you can give me
your collar now."

"But you didn't win," I cried indignantly. "I beat you
easily."

"I won all the same," she asserted. "I always win because
I am Pharaoh's daughter."

I made a sign to protect us and stood trembling. "Don't
say such things," I implored her. "Pharaoh is a god, and
nobody jokes about him. How dare you tell such lies in
any case? Pharaoh doesn't live here."

"He wouldn't live in a nasty little place like this with that
fat woman," she said furiously, tears gathering in her eyes.

"All right, then, if you were his daughter, you certainly
would not be here."

She struggled for speech for a moment, swallowing
rapidly and clutching the gold sign on her breast. "My
father has a holy sickness," she began at last. "A god enters
into him sometimes, and when this happens he cries out and
falls to the ground, struggling terribly. At last when the
god has mastery over him, he lies still and sees strange
visions, but when he awakes from these, he is very ill."

"Everybody knows that about Pharaoh," I remarked in
skeptical tones.

"Well then, today as we came to see the new temple my
father is building, we drove by chance down the street
which runs past this miserable house. Suddenly my father
gave a great cry and rolled out of his chariot. My mother

jumped down with a shriek, calling to our attendants, who took him up and carried him immediately inside. No one waited for me, but I went in too and saw a fat woman, smelling like these bushes only worse, who was running around screaming out orders to her servants. I did not like her at all, and nobody noticed me, so that I went out into the garden by myself. They may find me if they can."

"They will be looking for you everywhere," I said in a terrible fright, knowing that it would be as much as my life was worth to be found with her here.

"Let them," she said sulkily. "What do I care?" She turned away from me and began twisting a flower off the bushes. "The holy sickness frightens me," she said after a pause, and I saw her shoulders heave in a sob.

I came up and stood behind her in silence, not quite daring to touch her. She began to sob harder, but still not very loud. "Here, take my luck charm," I said desperately, dangling it up and down in front of her face. "It is very powerful for bringing good luck in our family, and who knows what it may do for you? See the red signs to hang down your back against devils! I expect you will feel better if you will only put it on."

She looked at the luck charm for a minute and then turned around and flung her arms about my neck. I did not venture to hold her, but stood stiff like a post, though I liked the feel of her soft cheek against my shoulder and the scent of her dark hair. "If I take your mother's luck charm," she said at last, "you must have mine." With that she lifted off the heavy collar and flung it over my head.

There was a yell from behind as someone crashed through the bushes to grab me before I could slide out of the little girl's arms and duck away. I kicked out as best I could and bit savagely at his hand, but the fellow began cuffing me until I was dizzy, and then twisted up my arm till I screamed. He laughed at that and hit me again while he forced me through the bushes into the open space beyond.

"A street boy, mistress," he called, "with his hands on the princess. I got to him just in time."

A great fat woman came lumbering up the slope from the pond, her wig fallen a little sideways, and her big arms working like oars as she tried to run. Her servant held me fast for her, while she beat me about the head until my face was covered with blood from the marks of her heavy rings. "How dare you," she panted, "raise a hand to the princess. Take that! And that! It's nothing to what you'll get later. And that!"

"Let him alone," yelled the princess in a passion, beating at the fat woman with a branch she had torn off one of the flowering bushes. The fat woman stopped hitting me for a moment to protest.

"Why, Princess Merytaton," she exclaimed, "the boy has stolen your collar, and perhaps might have taken your life. Young villain!" She struck me again.

"He SAVED my life!" screamed the princess frantically, "and you'll be sorry for having dangerous things in your garden."

"What was in my garden?" asked the fat woman in puzzled tones, turning away from me to stare in astonishment at the angry little girl.

Princess Merytaton looked around a little wildly for inspiration, and her eye fell on the tiny pond overgrown with water lilies. "A crocodile," she asserted loudly.

"A *crocodile?*"

The Princess Merytaton nodded and looked the fat

woman straight in the eye. "A great big crocodile came up out of there," she said solemnly, pointing at the inoffensive little pond which even a large frog would have been ashamed of. "He was going to eat me, too, but this boy frightened him away."

"But — "

"You think I am telling a story, don't you?" demanded Merytaton. "Well, I can tell much better stories than that when I want to, and my mother believes them. There was a slave we had once who teased my puppy. I told my mother a story about him and made them have him killed. I expect they will kill you too if you don't do what I say."

The fat woman crumpled completely. "Princess Merytaton," she said imploringly, "if you wish me to take this boy in and tell the wife of divine Pharaoh that he saved your life from a crocodile in my frog pond, I will certainly do it. Nevertheless, I imagine that Pharaoh's wife may suppose some god has driven me mad."

"Of course we won't take him in," declared the princess, shaking her head with great emphasis. "We are going to put him back over the wall, so there!"

"But the wall is far too high."

"There is always a place in a wall where the slaves sneak out at night," asserted the princess. "They don't like me to know, but I find out, and I don't tell as long as they do what I say. Make this fellow show us."

The servant let go of my arms and hesitated, turning uncertainly from one to the other. "I think — I — I have heard — a rumor," he stammered, rolling his eyes in an agony of fright.

There was a shady tree by the wall in the corner, not very

tall, but well grown and climbable. Above it, the slave boy asserted, I should find handholds knocked in the wall.

"Goodbye, boy," said Merytaton as I laid my hand on the tree trunk. "I wish I could kill all these grownups and come and play with you in the street." She flung her arms about my neck once more and pressed her warm lips against my cheek. I endured it, trembling slightly, for the blood of the gods which ran in her veins is a terrible thing. With his mere nod, Pharaoh can send hundreds to death if it pleases him, and Merytaton, who was younger than I, was already familiar with these things. I went up that tree, when she released me, much faster than any tree was ever ascended before.

"Stop!" shouted the fat woman behind me. "Come back! Throw down the princess's collar. Stop, thief!"

"I gave it him," I heard Merytaton answer, "and I want him to keep it. I expect that I shall tell my mother you stole it, and I wonder how you will like that."

For my part, I was clinging to the wall like a fly at that moment. When I reached the top and turned round, Merytaton was already running back to the house with the fat woman panting behind and calling out to her. The hoarse voice grew fainter and fainter with distance and breathlessness. I saw the red signs of our luck charm flapping on Merytaton's back as she ran. She disappeared behind a tree, and I turned and slid over the wall.

It was dark when I got home, but Mother had actually lit a lamp to wait for my coming. I could see that for some reason or other she had been in tears. "You wicked boy, where is my luck charm?" she screamed, darting immediately for the corner in which she kept a useful stick. She reached

across and grabbed me by the forelock, but as she did so, her
eye fell on the collar, glittering even in the pale rays of our
smoky lamp. She made a hoarse choking sound in her throat,
let go my hair, and put her hand up to her mouth. For the
first and only time I saw my mother speechless, though as a
general rule she was a woman who did not lack for words.
It was my father, usually so silent, who asked me, "In the
name of Aton, boy, where did you find that thing?"

My mother simply sat on the cornbin and stared at me,
nor when I had told my story did she for once have any ideas.
It was my father who decreed that we should take our few
goods in our hands and steal down to the water. He arranged our passage in a trading vessel that was going up the
water to Thebes. The captain, like all Thebans, was a wor-
shiper of Amon who hated the new god of Pharaoh and the
city being built. For this reason he asked no questions about
why we fled from it. Once we were hidden in the vast city
of Thebes, we felt more safe from Pharaoh's eyes. Father
took a few pieces of the collar and bought us a house with a
yard and a sycamore tree to sit under. He also bought slaves
skilled in making clay figures such as rich men put in their
tombs to be their servants in the land of the dead. From the
earnings of these, he prospered moderately, so that my
mother had women slaves to do her washing and grind her
corn. She still went to market, however, where one day she
purchased a quantity of bright blue beads, red yarn, and gold
thread.

"What this family needs is a luck charm," she said in her
positive way. "We will take it to the temple when I have
made it, and we will buy a big offering for Amon in return
for his blessing."

This we did, and pieces of the princess's collar still lie buried under our floor, for our good fortune continued. When I die, my children may divide them as they will. The luck charm will go to the third of my sons, who is strongest and handsomest of all.

4

THE FIRST-BORN

I WANT SOME! I want some!" Riki tugged at his mother as the servant was offering roast goose so that a piece of breast slid off the platter, down Aset's spotless linen dress, and onto the floor. A near-by servant dived for it in shocked silence, while the steward beckoned hastily for another to come running forward with water and towels. Riki shrugged his shoulders a little sulkily and began to study the bright pattern of flowers on the tiled floor, which was painted to represent a garden. On ordinary days he would now have been sent from the room, especially as he was not supposed to speak while music was playing. However, Aset had not forgotten the occasion, and she only smiled as she beckoned the girl back and picked out a drumstick.

"Don't get it all over your face, then," she warned, handing it to him.

Riki felt insulted. "Of course not," he swaggered, taking a dainty little nibble. "I am too big to do that any more."

"After one morning's school?" inquired his father, signing to the harpist to leave off and taking up his cup from the little table beside him. "What did you learn there that makes you so grown-up?"

There was a flying heron in the frieze around the wall to which Riki always looked for inspiration when he was troubled by questions. He lowered his bone and glanced up at it, screwing up his eyes in an effort to remember correctly. "The ear of a boy is on his back," he chanted in a nasal singsong, rocking a little. "He listens best when he is beaten."

Pharaoh's captain, who was the guest of honor, roared loudly, throwing back his head and opening his mouth to show his teeth. "I suppose you were beaten after that?" he asked, fingering the collar of gold which Pharaoh had given him when he appointed him to take charge of the frontier forts.

"No," conceded Riki, reluctant to lose importance by the admission. "Not today. Puamra was beaten, though, and he howled ever so loud."

The captain roared again while Riki, who was not used to being laughed at, fidgeted angrily, resisting a temptation to cry. Riki's father came to the rescue as he so often did. "Always howl before you are hurt," he agreed solemnly, "and perhaps the master will not hit you very hard. What else did you do?"

"I learned how to mix ink," said Riki, who had forgotten his good resolutions and was covering himself from nose to chin with grease. "I had a piece of an old pot to write on, and I painted marks on it for hours and hours." He sighed. "When can I leave school? I don't really think I like it."

"It is a long time to sit still, especially at first," agreed Nebamon sympathetically. "How would you like to hunt birds in the marshes this evening for a change?"

"Hurray!" Riki began to jump and clap his hands, dropping the bone, which was picked up by a slave and disposed of in a basket. Fruit was offered.

"Riki!" said Aset, noticing, "go over and get your face washed, you messy boy. You had better go to your rest at once if you are to hunt."

"I want to stay and see the dancers," protested Riki without moving. "I know all the dull old stories the tutor tells at rest times anyway. I wish — " One of the servants had taken him by the hand, and he could see that his mother was not smiling. Prudently he let his voice die off into a loud muttered grumble as they led him away.

Aset raised her lotus flower to her nostrils and looked over it apologetically at Pharaoh's captain. "We spoil the child because he is our only son," said she.

"We do indulge him," agreed Nebamon smiling, "but the schoolmaster will teach him obedience with a stick before very long. Meanwhile, shall we see these dancers? They are Syrians and such as you will often meet if you go to command the frontier fort."

"That is so," agreed the captain sourly, "and I must admit that I like the acrobatic dancing of the Egyptians better than all this foreign bending and swaying. Give me a woman who can turn a somersault backwards in time to the music, or walk on her hands. I have no use for Syrians."

Nebamon seemed a little put out at this frank admission, but he judged it best to go on with the entertainment and made signs accordingly. However, as the mandolins began to strum rhythmically and the Syrian women grouped themselves, posturing between the painted pillars, his politeness moved him to pursue the conversation, lest the captain find his hospitality tedious.

"The captain of Pharaoh's fortress may be far from his master's sight," began he pleasantly, "but he need never be absent from his mind. Many embassies entering with tribute

may bear with them respectful greetings from the keeper of
Egypt's gate. These dancers themselves have come in past
the fortress and will be all the fashion in Thebes a month
from now. Such people are glad to mention the man who
has given them a pass, and they will drop a word here and
there in season which may bear fruit in time to come."

The captain, whom wine was making quarrelsome, scowled
at a platter which a young slave boy was offering and pushed
it aside. "Syrian fruits!" he said contemptuously, "and Syrian dancers! If I had my way, such trash would never enter
the country except as prisoners. No, I know a far better
road to promotion than such mean forms of currying favor."

"And that is?" Nebamon was angry, but as a host he had
determined to remain polite.

The captain put out a finger and poked Nebamon in the
ribs, causing him to start away irritably. "Not the people
coming in," he said with a chuckle, leaning over and placing
a sticky hand on the carved arm of his host's chair, "but the

people going out!" He smiled in a satisfied fashion as though
he had said something very clever. Nebamon was mystified.

"The people going out?" he repeated. "Embassies of
Pharaoh?"

The captain winked. "Not the embassies, young fellow,"
he said with patronizing self-confidence. "The criminals!"
He held out his cup to be filled and nodded to himself.

Nebamon felt a twinge of disgust. "Oh, criminals!" he
responded coldly. "Most runaway slaves will die in the
desert if they do get past the gate. However, please yourself
if you think they are worth catching."

The captain bent forward again and lowered his voice to
a hoarse confidential whisper, which was nevertheless perfectly audible over the sound of the music. "What do you
say to a Syrian escaping from Pharaoh himself?"

"A slave of Pharaoh's? Why, he has thousands and will
not even thank you for recovering the man."

"This is no slave but a Syrian actually brought up in the
palace who has reverted to type, as they all do, and has killed
an Egyptian. Bad blood will out! I must press on tonight
as soon as my chariot is ready, for Pharaoh really wants to
catch this Moses, and I would miss a great chance if he were
to sneak out into the desert before I arrived."

The Syrians were ending their dance, and Nebamon took
the opportunity to push back his chair. "Personally," he said,
"I am happier laying traps for birds instead of men. However, my carpenters are repairing your chariot, and when
you have slept, we will both go hunting, you in your fashion,
and I after mine."

"If you had ever been out of the country and seen the
world," said the captain rudely, "you would know there is
nothing in it but Egyptians and worthless trash. It will do

me good to teach this Syrian that he is not a prince, as he has
been brought up to think."

"May all Pharaoh's enemies meet with such a man!"

"You and your Syrian servants!" retorted the captain,
working himself up into a passion at the mockery of Nebamon's tone. "I wonder if I could not hunt Syrians better by
staying here with you."

Nebamon started up so violently that Aset hurried to in-
tervene. "You must be careful in the boat this evening," she
interrupted quickly, laying a hand on her husband's arm. "I
am a little afraid because Riki had a bad dream last night."

"A dream? What dream?" Nebamon was fairly startled
out of his quarrel. "Why was not the soothsayer told?"

"He cannot remember it," replied Aset timidly. "Nevertheless, he screamed as he awoke."

"It is no matter then." Nebamon shrugged and turned
more calmly to his guest. "The slave will take you to your
room, and after that I will wish you a very good hunting,"
said he.

The first day of school had really been tiring, and Riki
fell asleep during the tutor's story, only waking in time to
rush out to the stables and get in the way of the servants
harnessing Nebamon's chariot. The head groom, who was a
deliberate old fellow and disapproved of Riki, could by no
means be hurried. "The master's guest has not yet taken
leave," grumbled he, sending back a groom to the stable for
another strap.

"Bother the old guest!" shouted Riki, dancing with impatience and causing the horses to shuffle uneasily when he
came near.

By the time that Pharaoh's captain had been sped on his

way with fitting compliments, it was already late in the afternoon. Riki, who was only allowed to drive when the horses
were walking, unwillingly resigned the reins to his father for
the sake of speed. The chariot lurched clattering along the
raised bank that did duty both for a path and for a dyke to
control the flood waters of the canal. It was the height of the
growing season, so that slaves were working wearily at the
buckets, and little detours had to be made to cross the ditches
carrying water to the vegetable patches, the wheat, the vine-
yards, and even the gay pastures dotted with pink and yellow
flowers. Everywhere men were at work, slowly at first, and
then as the rattle of the chariot came to their ears, with
furious activity. Farm laborers began to hoe frantically at
weeds, overseers yelled and laid about them, slaves splashed
water hurriedly into the ditches. In the tumble-down village
the women came to their doorways, throwing out spindles
before them as though their lives depended on not wasting
time. With shrieks their scrambling children deserted the
roadway, only to swarm back across it as soon as the master
was past.

Not far beyond the village, the canal had been artificially
widened to form a large shallow pond so much overgrown
that except at one end the water was chiefly visible in narrow
channels winding between matted islands of reed. Beside a
small landing place stood two servants, one holding the
curved throwing sticks of polished wood, the other waiting
by the boat, which was made out of tarred rushes bound
round a shallow wooden core. Riki scrambled out of the
chariot and jumped into it, amusing himself by rocking from
side to side while Nebamon was taking the sticks and throwing off his upper garment.

"Quiet now, Riki," he said, taking up the light paddle and beginning to move the boat very gently across an open space scattered with water-lily leaves and yellow blossoms.

The pond was not very noisy, and there was little to be seen, yet it was evident that the reeds were alive with birds. A heron rose from the far corner and sailed off. A moment later a vast flock, disturbed perhaps by its whirring wings, decided to shift their quarters. They rose by hundreds, circled awhile, and dropped back into the rushes nearer to the oncoming boat than they had been before. Nebamon, who had halted a moment, standing perfectly still, now dipped his paddle cautiously in the water and began to move again.

Presently he took up two or three sticks and handed back the paddle to Riki, who held his tongue between his teeth and breathed heavily in an effort not to splash. Half a dozen birds flew up on either side as the channel narrowed, but Nebamon was far too experienced to let fly at such inferior targets. In another moment the boat would  have to part the reeds and nose its way between them. Nebamon raised his right arm.

Almost immediately there was a frightened squawk ahead, and with a noise of thunder the whole air was suddenly full of birds. Nebamon let fly four times, heard the dull thud as his sticks made contact, and snatched hastily at the pile by his feet. A last duck dropped limply into the rushes, and the air was clear. "Where are they, Riki?" he called to the excited little boy, who was shaking the boat in perilous fashion behind him.

Riki knew that it was his duty to mark where the birds had fallen, but in the excitement he had forgotten to do so. "Over there!" he stammered, hesitating.

"That was the last one," agreed Nebamon, "but I saw him myself. Riki, Riki, you will never make a hunter until you learn to keep your head." He caught hold of the reeds and pulled the boat forward in the direction of his quarry.

The last duck was hanging limply in a mat of reeds, and the stick that had killed it was floating in the water ten yards off. No amount of pushing through the channels, however, could find the other victims, and Nebamon, who valued his throwing sticks, felt annoyed. "If we knew where they were," he complained, pointing out a spot where the tangle of reeds had formed a large matted island, "we might reach them from one side or the other. As it is, there is nothing to be done."

"Let me go and look," cried Riki, beginning to scramble hastily out of the boat.

"Get back!" shouted Nebamon crossly. "Those islands are all reed and mud," he added in a calmer tone as Riki withdrew his foot. "They are not at all safe, and they sometimes have snakes. We have lost so much time that unless we go on now, we shall not be able to give you a turn before dark. You had better come up into the front and stand ready while I take the paddle. Remember, an overarm throw with a good swing will set the stick whirling. It is not so important to aim as it is to throw really hard."

"You need not raise your hand yet," he cautioned in low tones as they crept across the open water. "The birds will be some way off, and you do not want to get tired."

Again they passed into the reeds, and this time because Nebamon was skillful, they were almost upon the flock before it rose. Riki clenched his teeth and threw. There was a squawk as something fell flapping. "Bravo!" shouted his father. "Throw again!"

Riki tried, but in his excitement, he forgot to let go until too late. His stick splashed violently into the water a yard in front of the boat, and before he could recover from his confusion, the birds were out of range. "Too bad!" said Nebamon laughing, "but I think your first shot hit a big one if we only can catch him. Those ducks can move quite fast with a broken wing."

The wounded bird cowering in the rushes had been marked down by Nebamon's experienced eye, and the boat drove directly for his hiding place. There was a short wild struggle as Riki clutched him, but with an agonized squawk it tore loose and flapped clumsily away. Riki made a fierce spring,  landed on a tussock, and went slipping and stumbling across the marshes in his wake.

"Come back!" shouted Nebamon, making a furious grab which threw him so far off balance that he teetered in the rocking boat and collapsed into the stream with a heavy splash. As he came up, he heard Riki yelling for help, and he well knew the treacherous nature of those islands of reeds and mud. It would take him some minutes to ease himself back into the light boat without upsetting it, and he would probably find no channel through which to force his way to Riki's side. Nebamon deserted the boat in frantic haste and made for the reed bank, hauling, sliding, grasping desperately at the yielding mud. Weed immediately entangled his arms, flies blinded him, half-liquid ooze clutched at his hands and feet. Progress was slow, but a hasty movement might cause him to stick in the mud while Riki perished, or even to drown himself before the servants could rescue him. Nebamon slid very cautiously sideways into deeper water and, shaking the mud out of his eyes, attacked the ooze once more.

"I have your boy," called out a man's voice, panting. "Get the boat quickly, though, for he is hard to hold."

Nebamon's surprise and relief at this unexpected aid were so enormous that it was only his own head going under water that brought him sufficiently to his senses to make an answer. "It will take time to fetch the boat," he spluttered at last, "but I will make all haste I can."

He found a man lying at full length across a tussock, with his arms out over his head supporting Riki and his face sinking into the water between them, except when he jerked it back to take in a gulp of air. Riki himself was so much entangled by weed that it was necessary to move cautiously around him and to tear off the stems by handfuls before he could be eased into the boat. He seemed dazed, and when he recovered, it was only to vomit up quantities of slime. Nebamon held him in his arms, while the stranger, still sitting in the mud by the boat, looked quietly at them as though he had not decided what he should do next. He was a powerful man, and it flashed through Nebamon's mind that a fugitive who hid in the marshes might be dangerous if he thought he was entrapped. The man certainly looked like a savage. Deep-set, dark eyes glared out of a bush of thick black stubble almost half an inch long. What could be seen of his face was swollen by horsefly bites into great lumps, from which here and there a trickle of blood was running. He sat in mud almost to the waist, flies swarmed on him, and he stank of decaying matter from the marsh. Yet his shoulders were unbent by toil and unscarred by beatings, while the ragged remains of his garment were as finely woven as Nebamon's own. A slave would cringe, but this man haughtily gave back stare for stare. There could be but one such fugitive in Egypt.

"Moses, the Syrian," said Nebamon with quiet assurance. "The murderer on his way to the frontier gate!"

"Not murderer, but avenger," corrected he with pride. "I made life pay for life."

"I also pay in this fashion," Nebamon assured him as he bent over Riki. "You must not go up to the frontier now, since all the patrols will have been warned. A captain left here for the fortress today, and he was in a great hurry to earn a reward from Pharaoh for capturing you." He grinned a little. "You had better come home with me and grow that fine beard you have started in Syrian fashion. In a month, when it looks better, we may smuggle you out with a party of traders going home. In the meantime, you may trust me to hide you, and to send a report around that you are dead."

"You are a born trickster, I see, like all Egyptians," said Moses coolly. "You enjoy an intrigue for its own sake. It is not my destiny to die in Egypt, but I have not your cunning and must be content that you are sly enough for us both."

Nebamon opened his eyes indignantly at this, but he made no motion to prevent Moses from entering the boat. It was Riki who drew aside his legs and turned his head on his father's arm with a whimper of dismay. Nebamon immediately felt ashamed that his son should shrink away from his rescuer. "He has probably never seen a man so badly shaven," he apologized with a little laugh.

"Children are always afraid of me in Egypt," said Moses as he reached for the paddle. "It is very strange, and I have never understood it."

It was already dusk in the shadow of the bulrushes, and the boat came out into the open water as the last edge of the sun was going down. The village street was completely empty by the time that the chariot clattered through it, for the laborers went to bed at sunset and used no lamps. Nebamon was well content to have it so and to find the path deserted, as he was aware that he ran some risk if he were seen with this strange passenger. It was with dismay that he saw a gleam of torches by his entrance gate and reflected that Aset must be sending servants to find out what had delayed him. However, since those in the house would soon learn of the Syrian's presence, it really mattered little if they saw him now. Nebamon was almost in the gateway before he perceived that with his servants stood a group of soldiers, such as he had sent away that very afternoon. He halted abruptly, but too late. Pharaoh's captain, whom he had thought far away by now, stepped triumphantly out of the shadows to greet him.

"Good evening!" said he in an exultant tone. "My instinct told me I should have good hunting here. I see that it was right."

Nebamon forced himself to shrug his shoulders. "It is always a pleasure," he said coldly, "to welcome a guest. This young man whom you seem to suspect is not, however, dangerous. He is only one of the Syrian musicians who went out of his wits, as they tell me, and wandered away."

The captain laughed rudely. "A likely story when the man comes home in your chariot, driving by your side. I would not care to be in your place when Pharaoh hears it."

"You want to take the fellow upriver, I suppose," replied Nebamon. "Do what you wish, since the dancers are going on to Thebes in any case. I have no time to stand here arguing while my child needs care. Take the fellow, and ask my steward where you can lock him for the night." He pushed roughly past the captain and departed, carrying Riki, whom he handed over to Aset. Immediately he sent his servants running for the youngest mandolin player in the Syrian troupe.

Nebamon's house, which was almost a village in itself, contained among the servants' quarters a small but stout jail with bare floor and walls and a tiny slit for a window, just big enough for the jailor to hand in food or drink. By standing with his head against this opening, Moses could see quite an expanse of starlit sky. This comforted him, for he was a lonely man in Egypt and could not feel akin to anything less remote. It was cold by the little window, and he was damp as only a man could be who had soaked in mud and water a whole day long. He shivered in the breeze, but he was happy because he was pondering strange and lofty thoughts. He did not fear the cruelties of Egypt, yet he longed for the silent desert where he might lose himself from human sight amid sand and stones and stars.

Someone was fumbling with the bolts, and as he turned, the door swung inward, grating a little. "Quiet," said the voice of Nebamon. "We have drugged the guard, but he might yet awake."

A strange young man whose hair and beard had been raggedly shorn now slipped in through the moonlit doorway without a word and curled himself in a corner as though he were asleep. "Your substitute," said Nebamon grinning, "a young Syrian musician. He is well paid and runs no risk, except of being roughly handled on his way to Thebes. He does not look very like you, to be sure, but I have not infinite resources. The captain has only seen you once, in a very poor light. I am almost sorry for the captain," he added with a satisfaction that completely belied him. "He should have known better, perhaps, than to lay a trap for me."

"And what ingenious scheme have you made for my future?" inquired Moses with a half-unwilling smile.

"You are to get on a donkey, which I shall give you, and to ride as fast and as far as you can before it is dawn. No warning has gone up to the frontier, for this captain who bore it was anxious to keep the glory of catching you all to himself. Long before he reaches Thebes with the musician, you can easily have scrambled over some unguarded place in the wall."

"Nebamon," said Moses slowly, putting out a hand to arrest the Egyptian as he turned away, "I am not ungrateful, but I feel that the very blood in my veins is alien to yours. I do not like your ingenious tricks, and I despise the malice which prompts you to make a fool of Pharaoh's captain. Instead of thanks, therefore, take this warning. I hate Egypt, and one day I shall bring ruin upon it if you are stupid enough to let me go."

"Syrian," answered Nebamon haughtily, "take away your dirty hand! I neither ask your thanks nor dread your warning, but simply pay what I owe for Riki's life."

"The price of Riki's life!" said Moses solemnly. "As such I take it. You may yet wish you had not paid me that."

5

THE BLACK MAGICIAN

I NEVER HAD any fear of my father's magic until the night when I stretched out my arm between his victim and the power of his curse. Such indifference came naturally to a boy born in the burial city, where countless charms were daily employed to provide an easy life after death. My father's powers meant no more to me than those of a painter who spends his life copying good-luck sayings in bright, clear bands of pictures around the coffins of the dead. To be sure, a high brick wall had been built to conceal our rooftop from the neighbors, and on some mornings I had found a heap of ashes up there and a strange, sweet smoke in the house. I slept soundly in those times and had no idea that quiet forms used to steal past me on nights when the moon was full, groping carefully for the ladder to our roof. Later on, when pain kept me awake, I often heard them, and I even learned to distinguish by smell between the trades to which Father's invisible customers belonged.

I had always lived in the burial city, and it was a commonplace to me that every craft there was connected in some fashion with the service of death. A clean scent of wood shavings must mean a coffinmaker. A whiff of dried smoky

earth would be a potter fresh from taking a tall funeral jar
or a batch of little glazed amulets out of his oven. A stuffy
smell of dried flax clung to the weaver, who made coarse
linen wrappings to swathe the bodies of the dead. These and
many other such workmen held no special terrors. It was on
nights when more sinister people felt their way up the ladder
that I needed to cover my ears against the sound of muttering, and to roll my head in the rushes until I could hear
nothing but the beat of my heart and the heavy throb of
blood in my injured arm.

On these bad nights I smelled out gravediggers from the
slave gangs up in the hills, possessors of strange secrets about
hidden rock tombs where rich men lay buried with their
treasures. These people were dirty, sweaty, and frightened,
since to be caught outside their quarters meant death. With
them mingled the sickly odor of embalmers, who were all
known to be corpse robbers, and whose dreadful trade had
bred in them a contempt for the vengeance of the dead men
they despoiled. Most terrifying of all to me was an occasional clean, fresh smell of Nile weeds and water, betokening
a priest who must wash his whole body in the river three
times a day. When such a man, brought up amid magic,
came to need spells from Father, I felt as though the spirits
floating in the incense grew strong enough to stifle me.

Strangely enough, in the daytime Father was not a par-
ticularly sinister figure. He slept a good deal, and when I
saw him in the evenings, he seemed usually just a little drunk.
I never knew anybody who could consume so much beer as
Father, especially when the moon began to wane and the
house was full of offerings earned by his magic on the roof.
At these times there was a rivalry between my parents,
Mother rushing off to market with what she could snatch,

and Father ambling gently away with what he could hide to
pay the brewer of beer. Thereafter until his credit ran out,
he would spend the greater part of his waking hours in the
beer shop, coming home in the cool of the evening, slightly
mellow and in good humor for play. For all his great size,
Father had extraordinarily neat fingers and had modeled me
a clay doll with jointed legs, a cat arching her back, and a
duck with her ducklings behind her and her beak cocked
proudly in air. On the occasion when my story starts, he
had made me a crocodile with a jaw that would open and
shut realistically at the pulling of a string.

"Come on," he said when we had tired of watching it
gobble up the sort of people we disliked.

I picked up the crocodile and followed him happily, knowing that we were off to Hapu's workshop in search of paint.
Old Hapu made little models of houses, granaries, boats, servants, and other important possessions that a man might
want to take into the next life with him, but could not ac-

tually be walled up in his tomb. He and Father had a real interest in toys, and whenever I got a new one, we used to take it over and decorate it in Hapu's workroom. Old Hapu always said his overseer would never miss a little paint. He might have felt differently, had he known that when he was doing gilding, tiny crumbs of gold would disappear under Father's agile fingers and would find their way eventually to the beer shop when supplies at home were low.

Old Hapu was not working, which was unusual, and he looked ill. His small wrinkled face had fallen in somehow and had taken on deeper lines. He scowled as we appeared in the doorway and put up his hand in the gesture that is used to ward off the evil eye. "Leave me alone, Yuf the Magician," he said in a low hissing tone, glancing around at the corners of the little workshop as if he thought his dolls might possibly overhear. "Go away and leave me alone before I make trouble."

Father laughed scornfully, putting his hands on his hips in a swaggering fashion. "You are going to be rich," he said, "and work for yourself instead of for the temple. Why should you make trouble?"

"I tell you — "

"Now look here," said Father wearily, "how often do I have to repeat that nothing can possibly go wrong. The Mayor of this city will take his cut, while the officers of justice and the armed guards who police the Valley of the Tombs will all have theirs. As for the slaves in the grave-digger gangs, they are afraid of me." He touched a little green amulet which he wore around his neck and smiled.

"I am frightened too," said Hapu, whose hands were shaking. "I am afraid for my own skin. Look here!" He pushed aside the light bench on which he did his painting and showed

Father a small jagged hole bored through the wall. "Can you see where my wretched Syrian servant lay listening as I made arrangements to dispose of the gold when it should come? Does it surprise you to hear that he has fled?"

"Not in the least," said Father firmly, though I could see that he was somewhat startled nonetheless. "If he had asked us for a share of the treasure we shall steal from a dead king's tomb, we would certainly have killed him. He is welcome to try and see if he fares any better with the Mayor."

"He has not gone to the Mayor," cried Hapu in a sort of subdued scream, curving his hands into claws and shaking them before my father's face. "He has gone over the river to Thebes, whose governor is jealous enough of our Mayor to take the story to Pharaoh. This robbery was your scheme, Yuf the Magician. Now since you are so clever, tell me why I should not hurry after my servant and save my own neck by confessing what I know."

Father made no answer to that, but he slid his big hand quietly across the workbench and picked up a knife which Hapu generally used for slicing his little paintbrushes out of strips of reed.

Hapu skipped nimbly behind the bench and stood there, his hands resting upon it as though he were preparing to dodge a blow. "Do you think I am such a fool," he babbled hastily, "as to enter into a plot with Yuf the Magician and make no provision against sudden death? Too many others have made that mistake, my friend. If I die violently, a letter will go to the Governor over the river to tell him the name of a brewer of poisons who has customers from the very palace of the king."

"You know too much to die, Hapu, maker of models," said Father quietly, putting down the little knife in the exact spot whence he had taken it up. "Though you shall not die, however, you shall often wish you had. Send my name over the river if you dare, for I too have friends in the palace, and I think you may soon discover that my arm is long." He turned away, striding down the street so fast that I had to run after him, clutching the unpainted crocodile tightly in my hand.

Mother met us with a torrent of scoldings because when she had safely departed for market, Father had taken her purchases of the previous day and swapped them for beer. "You good-for-nothing, lazy, thieving rascal," she yelled, lunging for him with her broom. Father brushed her aside like a buzzing fly and went straight to his magic box, which lay along the inner wall.

Father's magic box was of battered but stout wickerwork, and it was always tied with a thong of leather and sealed over the knot with a wax impression of the curious green amulet Father wore about his neck. Never before had he opened it in front of me, and I tiptoed as close as I dared to get a view of the contents by the light of our sputtering lamp. Like everything else about Father, it was prosaic enough at first view. There was a brightly burnished copper bowl with strange signs scratched upon it, and a knife of a dark metal called iron, which was very rare and came from the north. There were a few jars of evil-smelling liquids, a bowl of a dark brown, crumbly substance which I knew was incense, a very big, blackish lump of wax, and several pieces of wire. Father pushed these aside and began feeling in the bottom for various little packets wrapped in fragments of linen, many of which I had seen and examined before.

One of the unexpected things about Father was his friend-ship with barbers, which was the more surprising in a man whose favorite economy was to shave himself. Every time that the full moon came round, Father gave away some part of his earnings to barbers, though as a rule the first thing that I knew about this was that one of them would slip a small package for him into my hand. Father never made any secret to me about the fact that he was collecting hair, and when I asked him why he wanted it, he laughed and said openly that it was good to have some sort of power over people with whom one had business dealings. Hair was very important in the making of magic, and I wondered very much what sort of thing Father would be able to do with Hapu's.

Father took out the wax and began to knead a small lump of it within his palms. When it was warm enough, he pressed it upon the sign which he wore on his breast, took it off again, and held it out to me. "Here, boy," he said, "take that down to the brewer of beer and tell him that I need a black dog to sacrifice this night around moonrise, and that he must not fail."

Mother snatched at the seal. "Let me go for him," said she. "Did you not promise the boy should be brought up as other boys are?"

Father put out his hand and detained her. "Does one night make him a magician?" he asked. "This rite must be secret, yet you know very well that no woman can hold the bowl for me."

I think the first moment in which I felt dread of my father's magic came when I took a squirming black puppy into my arms from the hands of the brewer of beer. It was so very small to leave its mother, and I had to keep dodging my head from side to side as it tried to lick my cheek. "It is ten days before full moon," the man had grumbled. "Tell

Yuf I was not ready, for such dogs are hard to find."

I nodded and started to walk back rather slowly, for I was wondering if the little dog would very much mind what must be done to it on our rooftop that night by the light of the moon. The little dog did mind, and I was glad when Father tossed its limp body into the shadows and took from my hands the copper bowl in which I had caught its blood. The moon was small, but myriad stars like blazing eyes crowded rank behind rank in the mysterious sky, as if their owners were staring silently at our piteous sacrifice. Father rose to his immense height and raised the bowl so that a little wind might carry the smell of blood to unseen nostrils. I crouched by the fire and scattered incense, whose green

smoke coiled about Father's limbs, making his head and hands dimly visible as though a great way up in the air.

A little log flaring on the fire was casting strange shadows. There was an indistinct mass behind Father, a small crouching lump beside me, and a flickering shape like a dancing man by the little wax image of Hapu, which Father had modeled to the sound of spells, kneeded with the old man's hair, and moistened with the blood of the sacrifice while it was warm. The round shoulders, thin neck, and peering little head of the doll were so like old Hapu that I thought of him and myself together as shriveled to pygmies, while Father had reached into the heavens and spoke with the watchers behind the stars.

Far away up in the smoke, Father called aloud on the fearful name of his demon. Its howling sound went echoing off into the dark and disappeared, as though swallowed up in the distance by a host of listening ears. Away in the eastern hills, a jackal made answer. Father poured a dark splash from his bowl to the ground, and called once more.

I got up, shaking, to my knees and lifted Hapu, for the time had come when I must hold the old man while Father did to him the things he wished to do. The incense was all burned away, and though smoke still hung in the heavy air, I could see Father's face come down into the firelight, glowing coppery red and dreadfully streaked with the painted marks which were the signs of power. Father's hands were red as he thrust the point of his thin wire between the coals. His mouth was black as he called on the little wax image by the warmth of the blood and by the hair kneeded into its breast to be Hapu indeed.

I held Hapu, lest he struggle, while Father brought the red-hot point of his wire very slowly toward Hapu's cheek.

Hapu said nothing, but a wax tear of agony gathered in his eye and started downward. Suddenly I felt I could bear no more. With a cry, I threw Hapu from me, and felt the sting of the burning wire across my forearm as I moved. Father roared like the demon himself, and with that I screamed, got clumsily up from my knees, and made a rush for the ladder leading into the warm, friendly darkness of the house.

I thought that devils were behind me, and so they may have been. I only know that something caught my foot and that I came rolling down the whole length of the ladder and hit the ground with a fearful crash. I remember hearing my arm snap under me, but the rest of the night is a confusion of lights and pain and sobbing until I was wearied out and could cry no more.

Then passed a long period of pain, during which I noticed little, save that the full-moon sacrifices went on as before, though there was talk of the gang lying low until trouble died down. Father left the house most nights, but was cautious about appearing in the streets before dark. I would not go out myself, even when I grew stronger, lest the street boys jeer at me for being a cripple when they saw my useless, twisted arm. Father and I would sit together for hours in absolute silence, he drinking his beer, and I scratching moodily on the earthen floor with a pointed stick. I had my own thoughts, and they seemed to fill my days. I did not wonder about Father's, except when he looked at me for very long, as he would sometimes do when my strength returned.

Mother busied herself with the affairs of the house, and she would scold over trivial matters in her usual way. Never would she address any special word to me until the evenings when Father had sauntered to the doorway, looked up the street and down, and glided out like a cat who had business in the dark. Mother would come over to my mat, feel my head, and offer me some water. Then she would sit cross-legged beside me telling long tales of Memphis and her life there when she was young. They were always the same, these stories of her father, the artist in the temple of Ptah, of her brother, and the workshop where they lived. She would describe the wharves of Memphis, the market places, the streets, as though these things had some importance in her mind. I might listen, or I might fall asleep. She never asked me if I cared to hear these details or suggested, except on one occasion, they were my concern.

It was on a hot night when my arm was aching worse than usual that I made my first effort to be rid of her tiresome repetitions. "What do I care about artists?" I told her pettishly, "one-armed and good for nothing as I am?"

"The best apprentice that my father had was a one-armed man," she answered swiftly. "It is dexterity, not strength that matters in his trade."

I sulkily answered nothing, for I was half drowned in self-pity and preferred to think of myself as useless rather than to be aroused. Mother showed me a little amulet which she always wore, made of twisted gold wire and green glass beads. "For the price of a thing like this," she said deliberately, "any boatman would take you down to Memphis, son."

I simply sat there in silence until she sighed and took back her little charm, but on mornings when Father regarded me too closely, I used to find relief in picturing the streets of Memphis in my mind. I was sunk in helpless apathy which might have lasted forever, had not action been forced on me at last from either side.

One morning when I woke up, I found paints and reed brushes set ready for me, and beside them a little boat delicately modeled in baked clay. It was a copy of the most beautiful boat I had ever seen, the funeral barge of the Pharaohs, which was used to bear the coffins of dead gods over the river to their secret tombs in the hills. I could see the lotus flowers on stem and stern bending gracefully inward, the canopy of tiny palms, and beneath it the coffin carved with a dead man's face, his hands crossed peacefully. I reached eagerly for the paints, remembering the silver flowers, the gorgeous colors, and the gold. All morning long I sat absorbed in the delicate work, though I never said a word to my father, from whom I knew the present came. Still, I turned myself around so that he could see what I was doing, and he glanced across and smiled a little as he used to do at my playthings many months before.

Mother came bursting in from the street carrying a jar of water, which she put down in such a hurry that it splashed over the floor. "They have arrested the brewer," cried she before she had fairly got back her breath. "Four men came to take him away last night. I told you so!"

Father calmly dipped his long reed into the beer and took a pull on it. "I know you did," said he.

"There is a curse on this tomb robbery," cried Mother frantically. "Who are we to open a sealed rock chamber and take out treasures in which a king's spirit rejoices after death? First Hapu, and now the brewer! We shall all come to an evil end." She wrung her hands and hunched herself together as though in pain.

Father shrugged his shoulders with perfect indifference. "The brewer will talk, of course," he admitted, "but what of that? He knows the names of the guards who have been bribed and of the men who hollowed out the secret passage, but someone will see that he dies before he can confess too much. The Mayor must make some examples, but he still wants his portion of the treasure later on. Meanwhile, he protects me because I am to help him lay his hands on it."

"Can he not find other agents?"

"He may." Father hitched himself round on his mat a little so that he could lean back against the wall and look up into her face. "I have been thinking about that," said he, "but I have been waiting, for I did not want to escape without the gold." He glanced quickly at the doorway and lowered his voice. "We closed the secret passage with a rock when the Governor of Thebes began to make inquiries. It took six men to shift it, for we wanted to be sure that no one of us could enter and steal until things were safe for all. I have been sitting here many long months and wondering about that stone."

"Why?"

Father turned his head toward me and fumbled on the ground beside him for the hollow reed through which he drank. "We were hurried, and the rock was heavy to shift. It did not fit completely, so that we covered it with rubble and loose stones."

"Well?"

"I have been thinking that a small boy might wriggle through into the passage," said he.

I took my hand from the little boat, knowing now what Father intended to gain by playing with me. Mother rushed forward to my defense. "You swore that you would not use the boy again," she cried hastily, putting herself between us.

"Have you not done him enough harm as it is?"

"It is but for once, and this is not magic. Think of all the gold which we may never see without his help."

"I am thinking of all the times that you have promised to leave the boy alone."

"I follow my demon," said Father, "and what he bids, I do. If the child is a fitting instrument, I will never leave him alone."

There was a deep silence in the house. Father had shut his eyes to close the conversation and stretched his long length out against the wall. Mother went over to the water jar, lifted it wearily, and took it in to the back room where she used to prepare our food. Presently she came back and stood watching me at work, shuffling with her foot in the wet patch where the water had spilled. When she went away, I saw on the ground beside me her little amulet. As I went on painting, my hand moved steadily, though I understood her sign. We had been waiting, Father and I, each thinking his own thoughts through long months of silence. Now the end had come for both of us because I was strong enough to do what I must do. I got up with the little boat in my hand and sauntered quietly over to view it in the patch of sunlight by the door.

Father's eyes were still shut, and he was breathing heavily, though more because of the heat than because he was really asleep. Still, I had been very quiet and he looked drowsy. I slipped out over the threshold and dodged round the corner of the street. It was in the middle of the day when the heat of summer is fiercest. A few dogs lay in patches of shadow, while here and there a shopkeeper lay dozing under an awning, keeping a sleepy eye on his wares. No one took

notice of a boy, unless it was the beggars who sat by the
walls on the shady side with their empty bowls beside them
and their red eyes blinking hopefully at the sound of passing feet. I ran for my very life through the baking city, with
my father's last toy and my mother's last present clutched
together in my hand.

6

THE JUDGMENT OF THE GODS

HIS LIFE, thought the old storyteller wearily, had been a hard one. When the floods were up over the land, he was to be found in the slums, singing songs, telling fortunes of a sort, and writing letters cheaply for poor folk who did not care if the flowery sentences he knew by rote expressed their meaning incorrectly. There was usually a lump of coarse dark bread available, sometimes with a handful of onions; and far more frequently than there should have been, there was beer. Sometimes there was a ragged bit of a cloak in which to wrap himself as he slept in the corner of a yard, or in a narrow alley where the feet of people coming home in the dark would stumble against him. He made a living of a sort, but not a good one, especially since he had grown too slow in his movements to help himself out by pilfering when he could not buy. Every year the street boys hustled him about more violently, the blind or crippled beggars grew more menacing, and the chattering slum dwellers showed less interest in his threadbare tales.

It was far otherwise in the countryside when the harvest was in, and the storyteller went round from one little mud village to another with his small lyre and his writing instruments across his back. The whole populace, children and all, would squat around him in the yard of the headman's house or the open square before the village jail. They would rock with laughter over his feeble jokes and call again and again for a favorite song. There were dried fish, and occasionally even figs to go with the dark bread, and there was always beer. He would spend the night in somebody's hut on a soft pile of rushes, and in the morning he found fortunes to tell or letters to be written. People would solemnly ask his advice about the marriage of their daughters, or listen to his judgment on their petty disputes. For a few months the storyteller was a great man in the country, until the peasants had eaten most of their supplies, and grinding poverty set in once more.

Unfortunately, none of these benefits could be obtained without walking. The storyteller groaned for the hundredth time as he looked at the muddy ditch beside him and wondered if he should scramble down the steep bank to cool his face. He had been detained by commissions and farewells until the sun stood high in the heavens, while the cheap little presents with which he had been burdened had proved too heavy for a poor old man. One by one, he had been forced to drop them regretfully into the ditch. To add insult to injury, he had been robbed, though one might have thought that a ragged old man with a lyre on his back would have been safe in broad daylight, and in the middle of a stretch of open fields. Perhaps he might have been, had he not seen a scrap of a bush in the ditch and gone down the bank to eat his lunch in its shadow and to sleep through an hour or two of the hottest part of the day.

He had hardly taken out his bread and sat down to dabble his feet in the water before a great, rough, muddy hand

gripped him firmly by the ankle. A huge man rose out of
the slime with a squelching sound and snatched greedily for
the bread. The storyteller staggered to his feet and tried to
be off, but the bank was steep and his strength but feeble. In
another moment his little tidbit of cheese had also vanished,
and the beer which had been so heavy to carry was fast dis-
appearing down the big man's throat. The storyteller
watched in trembling fascination, uncertain whether to try
to escape again.

The big man showed his teeth, what there were of them,
and said, "Grr!" deep down in his throat. The storyteller
clutched frantically at the bank, clawed his way up it, and
tottered off as fast as his legs would carry him down the
road.

The harvesting of the second crop was by no means over,
yet the fields were strangely empty. There was no one
working the swinging buckets which lifted water into the
irrigation channels, even though second crops could only be
raised by incessant labor of this sort. To his right along a
second, larger ditch, there lay a village, but the storyteller
was giving a wide berth to this on account of an unfortunate
incident last year. There was nothing for it but to continue
in a direction where he knew a welcome would await him,
even though he was uncertain if his old legs would carry
him so far in the heat.

The storyteller groaned again and cast a glance uneasily
behind him. Perhaps it might now be safe to go down to the
water. He stopped, and as he did so he became aware of a
confused noise of shouts and screams ahead.

Many people seemed to be yelling at once, and this was
curious, since peasants did not collect together in a body
during the middle of the working day. Besides, it was the

period of midday heat when all who could afford the time were resting, while those who were not had no extra energy left to make a noise. The storyteller forgot his own past wrongs for the moment while he thought rapidly over what he knew about the village in front.

It was a little larger than the usual huddle of mud huts and possessed a fly-blown market square where there were always a few people with bits of pottery or linen to sell, which nobody ever wanted to buy. Such as it was, it was a center for the country round about it, and at the moment it sounded very much as though there was a riot going on. The storyteller felt too old for such disturbances, and he saw no use in going into a place where the people were too busy to pay him attention. On the other hand, the village to his right was definitely unfriendly, and the robber was lurking somewhere between him and the place from which he had come. Perhaps it would be best to rest a little and drink some of that brackish water, while keeping his ears open for signs that excitement was dying away.

There was not a bit of shade in this part of the ditch. Even the rushes had been cut, and goats had eaten every tiny blade of grass along the bank. Still, the old man could drink, wash off the dust, and wet his headcloth. Sleep was impossible in such a sun, but he was better off than on the causeway. He squatted down in the water for a while and listened to the noise.

It was evident that the tumult was not decreasing as the sun went lower. On the contrary, it seemed if anything rather louder than before. When the old man reached the first small mud huts, each with its yard and familiar scattering of dingy playthings, he found them empty even of children. The entire populace was evidently on the square. The

storyteller, who had heard certain rumors in the city during
the last season, nodded to himself and shrugged resignedly.
There was to be a war, no doubt, and men were being seized
for the army. He might as well get back to the city if so,
for with the countryside in an uproar he could hardly ply
his trade. For the moment he must go on, however, because
he was hungry. Years ago this would not have mattered,
but things were more desperate with him now. If he was to
make his way back to the city, he must first be fed.

The village jail, facing on to the square, consisted of a
small yard completely surrounded by a high wall of sun-
baked brick. This had been given a coat of whitewash in the
distant past, which was faintly visible as a band around the
top of the wall, where it was too high for anyone to reach.
Below, it had been completely rubbed off or covered with
the sketches of village wits. In the center, flanked by two
small square towers, was the gateway, crudely but effec-
tively closed by a latticework of poles surmounted by a
palisade of sharpened stakes. Around this surged a mob of
people, mostly women, holding up various articles, waving
frantically, or simply yelling. Children of all sizes bobbed
in and out of the throng, screaming rhythmically, helped on
by various cuffs from desperate mothers who felt they could
not express their feelings without more noise. Now and
then a woman could claw her way half up the lattice, only
to be dislodged by a resounding whack delivered from somewhere inside. Occasionally one would fight her way back
through the throng, face red, dress half torn off, and bosom
heaving, while she shrieked more often than not at the top
of her voice.

Around the edges of the square, the crowd was thinner.
Older people were standing about or sitting cross-legged and

swaying back and forth to the tune of a regular wailing, which they could keep up without much effort for hours. Most of them held food on their laps, though they were not eating. It was good food, as the old man could see, and enough for several days. His mouth watered as he began to make his way among them, peering about in the hopes of recognizing somebody he knew.

A little side door at the foot of one of the towers popped open, and two small round men came tumbling out like peas from a bursting pod. They were exactly alike down to the smallest detail, except that one of them held a staff in his hand and the other did not. Each waggled a finger and screamed at the other, while with an even wilder howl those who were nearest made a rush for them. In a very few seconds there was nothing to be seen but a swirling crowd, around which the children hopped and cried as before.

The old storyteller, still hovering on the outskirts, saw a hand and half a shoulder appear between two struggling forms. With a sudden impulse, he caught hold and pulled. The owner of the hand followed him suddenly, so that they both staggered a few paces, tripped, and fell to the ground with a crash.

"Ugh!" gasped the storyteller, confusedly sorting himself out from his prize and blessing the swift glance which had told him who was the owner of that hand. One of the troubles of growing old is the difficulty of remembering names and faces, so important for a man who makes new friends or enemies daily. Twins, however, are rare, and these had been conspicuous in the village for a moderate amount of wealth, or what passed for such where all were poor.

"Good day to you, Keres, or Kames," he remarked.

"Keres, Keres," answered the little man mechanically, sitting up and feeling for his headcloth, which had dropped off, exposing his naked head, badly shaven and ringed by tufts of spiky hair. His face fell ludicrously as he realized his loss and began to peer around him. At this point his eye fell on the storyteller, and he sat up with a start. "The storyteller!" he said with pleased surprise, instantly dropping his voice and adding gloomily, "Nobody wants to listen to your stories now."

"Is it recruiting?" asked the storyteller sympathetically.

Keres nodded. "They came about sunup," he said, "and we had not been warned in time to send our young men away. We shall never see any of them again!" He began to rock himself back and forth and to pour dust on his head.

The storyteller did not contradict him, knowing very well that the army never did release soldiers unless they were crippled, and that few of these conscripts survived longer than a year or two. "But surely the village has a quota?" he said in consoling fashion. "They will not take them all."

Keres stopped rocking, but hunched his shoulders gloomily. "There is a quota," he admitted, "but it was fixed in the old king's time, in the good days when there was a busy market here. My brother Kames says he must find such numbers that he does not even dare to release my son. My son!" He put up his hands and began again to smear the dust across his face. Tears gathered in his eyes. "Ramses, my son!" he said.

"If Kames is the headman," agreed the storyteller, "he will be beaten with many blows unless he supplies his count of men."

"Do you suppose his son is among them?" demanded Keres bitterly. "Yet when I go to him, my brother and but an hour my elder, 'I must have one son or the other,' says he, 'if not Antef, then Ramses'; and with this he bids me be content."

"Why then, he has done much if you may keep Antef, while other men lose all."

"Antef!" exclaimed the other vehemently. "That fool! That clod!" His voice broke, and he swallowed with a visible effort. "See here, old man," he continued when he had somewhat mastered his emotion, "it sometimes happens that a man may have two sons, for one of whom his heart yearns terribly, while the other is but an ox, a useful beast. Give Antef work, no matter how heavy, and he will labor steadily from dawn to dark. Yet while he is swinging the water buckets, if he should chance to see a stray goat nibbling at the springing wheat, he will go on watering as he has been bidden, though the crop for which he labors is being eaten up before his eyes. So slow and heavy is he that even his wife scarcely knows that he can speak."

"Send Antef, then, and keep Ramses, whom you love so well."

"Alas!" cried the old man desperately, "I cannot. I looked for Antef among the prisoners, but he has disappeared."

He began to wail again, while the storyteller, who was hardened to other people's miseries, bethought himself once more of his own. "We can do nothing," he suggested, "while we both are weary. Besides, we have a day, or possibly two to make a plan before the young men are marched away."

Keres rose to the bait quite willingly. "Things may look easier when we have eaten and rested," he admitted. "Come with me, and Antef's woman may prepare us food, since she has no reason to run shrieking about the square."

The house of Keres was not pretentious, though larger than many in the village. It consisted of two rooms built of mud brick and so low that a tall man might have easily put his head through the light covering of palm leaves which formed the roof. A grotesque little image of Bes, the countryman's god of good luck, grinned from a tiny platform against one wall. For the rest, the front room was furnished with a corn-bin, a grindstone, and a few utensils, together with a number of sleeping mats which were surrounded with an edging of burrs to discourage scorpions. Outside in the yard there was the usual heap of fuel in the shape of dried cow dung molded into bricks, while a few dusty bushes and a straggling tree afforded protection from the sun.

Antef's woman, with two small boys clinging to her skirt, came out from the inner room with food and a skin of beer. She was bent from heavy loads like all village girls, but there was a steadiness about her look as though her youthful strength was not yet quite exhausted. "Did you hear news of

Antef, my father?" asked she in a low, clear voice of surprising firmness.

Keres shrugged his shoulders. "No one has seen him since he went out to work the buckets a little before dawn."

"To work the buckets!" exclaimed the storyteller, on whom a little food was having an invigorating effect. "Is Antef a big man whose teeth are jagged and broken? He lies in the slime of the ditch a little way upstream from the buckets, safe enough under an overhanging bush and needing nothing, since he took my bread and cheese to feed himself."

The woman made no answer to this reassurance, save to put up her hand to her mouth with a little gasp. Keres, on the other hand, began scrambling eagerly to his feet. "Then all is well," cried he with brutal cheerfulness. "We will send the soldiers to fetch Antef so that my brother may release me Ramses in his place!"

"No!" With a sudden, fierce movement the woman darted into the doorway where she stood ready for a struggle with anyone who tried to pass.

She was a big and powerful woman. Old Keres looked at her helplessly a moment, and then turned to the storyteller in bewildered irritation. "Teach me to reason with a woman who has born sons to a man! How is it possible that she should care for such an ox?"

"Even the ox can be faithful," cried the woman hotly. "Shall we sell him to the butcher, though it be our hour of need?"

"Better the dumb beast than the son of the house," retorted Keres, making a tentative step forward, but backing hastily as the woman lunged. "Speak to her, old man," he urged, "and tell her to mind her duty, which is obedience to her elders in the house."

The storyteller, who was chewing his way methodically through a lump of bread as hard as a brick and freely mixed with small pieces broken from the grindstone, made signs that his mouth was too full to answer, while he hastily considered what to say. It was his guiding principle in all disputes to make no enemies, or at any rate to be on the winning side. He could not afford to quarrel with Keres, who had influence in the village and might force him to avoid the place for years to come. On the other hand, two old men were no match for such a woman, even if he had not long ago ceased to love a fight. He sighed, feeling for the thousandth time that life was hard when one grew old.

"Let the woman speak first," he said finally, temporizing in the hope that her anger would spend itself in tears or in a rush of hasty words. He was disappointed, however, in her self-command.

"It was you yourself, old Keres, who chose me," she began defiantly, "telling my father that Antef needed a woman who would be wise enough for both. Now therefore let me speak for Antef, who is fit for nothing but the simple tasks which he has known all his life. If you let the soldiers take him, he will be beaten, not one day, but every day until he dies. He will be like an animal who does not know what his master wants from him."

"That may be," interrupted Keres, "and I am sorry for it. Nevertheless, Ramses will also die, if not under the stick, then of thirst in the desert, by pestilence, or at an enemy's hands. Since I am the father of these two young men, their lives are rightly mine. It is but just that I should save the one whom we most need."

"Let the gods give judgment," cried the woman from the

doorway. "Would it not have been Ramses who went out early in the morning if the gods had wished to save his life? Abide, then, by the judgment of the gods!"

"The judgment of the gods!" repeated the storyteller curiously. "It is a fine phrase and worthy of a woman who must be wise for two. Now did the gods repent of their judgment when they sent me to this house with news of Antef? Such matters, I think, are too hard for my poor brain."

The woman made no answer to that, but she straddled across the doorway with the air of one who did not intend to change her mind. The storyteller was forced to try a different tack. "Let us wait till morning," he suggested pacifically, "and ponder the matter. If tomorrow we cannot agree, there will still be time to argue before the soldiers march our men away."

"Then I will sleep across the doorway," responded the woman with quick suspicion, "and do you two lie tonight in the inner room."

The inner room was even smaller than the outer one, and it was encumbered by the round and sooty hearth on which the woman did the cooking for the house. Still, there were mats here also, and a lamp of sorts which gave out much smoke and a very evil odor. By its dubious light the little room looked very much like a prison, especially for old men who could not climb out through the flimsy roof. The tiny window, or rather smoke vent, was far too small to provide a way of escape. The storyteller wandered over to the water jar, put in a hand, and cooled his heated face. He helped himself from a plaited string of onions as he strolled across to squat by Keres, who had thrown himself down on a mat in furious despair.

"This wise woman is but a fool," said the storyteller contemptuously, "to think that she can match her country wits with mine."

Keres started violently, but the storyteller was quick to silence him with a hand across his lips. "Quietly!" he murmured. "Can you not hear the woman move? What message shall I take to your brother Kames, while you stay here and quiet her suspicions until day?"

"If you could but get out," said Keres in low tones, "a letter would be safest. It must not be known that my brother will do this favor for me."

The storyteller looked dubious at this suggestion. "Can Kames read?" he objected.

"How should he?" answered Keres simply. "There are scribes with the soldiers who do that work."

The storyteller still was reluctant, pointing out that letters sometimes went astray. "No more than messages," Keres argued, "and they are more secret. It would be best perhaps if you would go into the jail and speak with my brother there yourself."

The storyteller shuddered. "A man should stay out of trouble when he is old," said he. "I will write the letter for you if you will have it so." He turned to fumble in his pack for the materials which he always carried.

The woman in the doorway shifted and propped herself up so that she should not go to sleep. Let the old men burn the light if they pleased and sit grumbling together. They would have plenty of time to get tired of gossiping before the soldiers had marched away. Meanwhile, if they called out, nobody would hear them, since the neighbors were all encamped on the square. The sound of murmuring would keep her wakeful, which was just as well because her labors were heavy and the day had been long. When the light went out at last, she found herself nodding. Again and again her head fell forward on her chest and awakened her.

There was a loud yell from the inner room, followed by a crash and a sound of groans. The woman, recalled to her senses with a start, scrambled up and put out her hands to block the doorway. "What is it?" she called out sharply over the din.

"It is the old storyteller," answered Keres panting. "He fell in a fit and broke the water jar. A devil is in him."

"I will come," said she, reassured, and started across the floor, only to collide with her father-in-law in the darkness of the inner doorway.

"Stay out, you fool!" gasped Keres, pushing at her with both hands. "Did I not say there was a devil in the man? Light the lamp in the outer room and burn herbs before the image, lest the devil tire of the old man and seize upon your sons."

One of the children had already set up a wail, and the woman needed no urging. With trembling hands she lighted the lamp and made haste to kindle fire before the image, muttering what charms she knew while the room was filling with the aromatic smoke.

"Good!" cried Keres, appearing for a moment around the corner of the door. "Hear how the devil shakes the man as he feels our power!" He made a sign in the air and vanished within.

In very truth the struggles had increased to the point where they shook the house. Both children were now screaming at the top of their lungs, and outside a dog began to bark.

While the woman hurried over to hush her babies, all the dogs in town took up the matter, howling defiance at devils with all their might.

Quite suddenly all was over. With a great shout, the devil left the old man, who ceased thrashing and lay quiet without so much as a groan. The children hushed their wailing. The barking died gradually away to snarls. A cool little breeze from the inner room was already scattering the smoke as old Keres put out his head and gestured at the lamp. "The man lies quietly," he said, "as those do who have conquered a devil. Let us sleep while we can, for when dawn comes, there is much to be discussed." He went back into the inner room, and the woman could hear him straightening the story-teller's body on its mat.

The old storyteller chuckled in the darkness as he made his way down the causeway to the point where the irrigation ditch branched out from the big canal. It had been too easy. First there was the breaking of the water pitcher over the wall to soften the dried clay into its original mud. Then there was the hasty enlargement of the window under cover of the struggle, the flight through barking dogs to the village, the letter pressed into the hand of an incurious girl. Long before the woman discovered his absence, the soldiers should have seized their prey. The storyteller shrugged. He wished he felt perfectly certain that the scheme had succeeded after all.

A man need not read or write too well to pick up an occasional meal by writing letters for the poor. Some twenty sentences written in characters which he can learn to copy in youth will last him a lifetime, since one man's need is very like another's. When he becomes old, however, and his memory fails him, he begins to jumble together the pictures which were once distinct in his mind. As a rule,

THE JUDGMENT OF THE GODS

even this is not important, since he who sends a letter will usually blame the receiver for reading it wrong. But in this case — the storyteller quickened his pace, wondering uneasily whether or not the letter was clear. A notion struck him. "The woman was right after all," he said aloud with a chuckle. "The matter is left in this fashion to the judgment of the gods."

Another thought came to him suddenly and stopped him full in his tracks. "I might as well have sided with the woman," said he, "and saved myself this trouble. As long as I do not know how the letter was written, I shall never dare enter the village, lest Keres revenge on me the loss of his son."

7

THE UNQUIET SPIRIT

IN LIFE my mistress was a dutiful wife to Penamon. She was gracious to her servants and thoughtful of her children, yet even at that time there was no doubt that she had an unquiet spirit. If it had been possible to waste such wealth as Penamon's, one might have said that she was extravagant. At all events, there was no end to her jewels, her transparent dresses, and her alabaster vases of perfume. The splendor of her entertainments was the talk of the town. I have known her to have a summerhouse constructed for a single party and decorated from floor to ceiling by a famous artist, only to be pulled down again the very day it was first used. I have seen her take ladies fishing, with bent wire, for precious jewels, and heard her stake a priceless bowl on a single throw of the dice. For all her blue hair dyes, her wigs, her lip salve, and her earrings, she was never beautiful. To do her justice, she cared very little to appear so. To her, fashion or a new sensation was all.

Few dared speak of Neferamon's childhood, though an old man once told me that it was an exceedingly happy time. She was brought up among the daughters of that accursed Pharaoh who built a new city in which to worship

Aton, the one all-powerful god. Vengeance fell upon him, and ruin upon Egypt, so that it is no longer good to speak his name. Once in my mistress's jewel box, I came upon his token, a golden sun with arms for rays and many hands extended, in blessing. I was puzzling over the symbol when Neferamon saw me, and she boxed my ears so hard that the thing jerked out of my hand onto the floor. As I stooped for it, I saw that she was trembling, though she did not say a word. After that, I often wondered how much she thought of those far-off days and that strange god who shone on all.

Whatever her past may have been, it could not be suggested that Neferamon failed in the least part of her religious duties. She had been married too young to have been made a priestess of Amon, but her daughter was early sent to the temple and dedicated to that god. Always she went with her husband when he offered sacrifice and prayed that the spirits of his parents might be granted a share of the feast. At the time of the New Year when the god in his silver shrine went up the river, her boat was resplendent among those that followed him. In the special rites which women performed, her place was second only to the queen's.

If her heart was not in the worship of Amon, that god can have cared nothing, since he concerned himself only that his ritual was perfectly performed. Her husband was satisfied if she did her duty and never asked whether she loved him, being as he was, much older and wrapped up in his career. The little girl, as I say, had been given to the temple, while the boys were soon with their tutors or in school. Thus, though she was often gay, I never saw her happy. The strange thing is that she should have cared for life sufficiently to return after her death.

Her illness came upon her after one of her extravagant

parties, where fabulous wines and cakes made with exotic spices had been served. Dwarfish tumblers had performed, and supple Nubians had danced to the sound of flutes beneath a canopy of flowers. She had been at her most witty. In the little room where I waited for her, I could hear the shrill sound of her laughter. Afterwards, when I came to take off her wig, which was heavy with sweet-smelling ointments, she suddenly threw herself on her couch and said, "Let me alone for the moment, Nebtu. I cannot bear any more."

I withdrew, knowing well this mood of my mistress when she was wearied of every single thing under the sun. Later, when she had slept, I returned to find her burning with fever and in manner very strange. Once she spoke of herself as Neferaton, using her long forgotten and forbidden girlhood name.

There was nothing to be done but call a doctor, and one might be sure that in a household such as ours he would be the wisest of all the temple priests. Immediately he saw my mistress, he recognized that a devil had seized upon her and must be driven out before she could be healed. However, though he called upon all the great gods to threaten that evil spirit, it had taken such firm hold that none of them could frighten it away. The wise man made a clay doll to be a new home for that devil, and he kneeded charms into a ball and laid them under my mistress's head. He even mixed healing draughts, but dared not give them until the demon had left her after three days' time. By then she was too weak to swallow, and it was clear that she must die.

She was restless at the last as though she wanted something. Penamon took her hand, but she turned her head away. I moistened her lips with water, and she looked at me quite sensibly and said, "Neferaton. Aton."

"What was that?" said Penamon, leaning across her.

"Just muttering," said I, for I could not bring myself to pronounce the name of the accursed Pharaoh's god.

My mistress gave a loud sigh and died. Penamon stood up. He had been watching most of the night, and he looked very old. "I will send for the priests," said he, "and all things shall be well done. Do you lead the women in mourning, as the custom is."

Some had already raised a shriek and torn their garments, pouring on their heads the dust of turquoise with which the floor of my mistress's chamber was strewn. I too cried aloud, and we rushed out into the streets with violent clamor, arousing the neighbors, and even strangers, to honor our dead. All through the best quarter of the town we lamented her, howling, disheveled, and streaked with the turquoise dust

and sand from the road. This was our duty, yet as I wailed, I found myself thinking, "Death is at least a new sensation for one who was weary of the sun."

There were seventy days of mourning while her body was in the hands of the embalmers, since for such a one as Neferamon every possible rite must be done. During all that time Penamon neither bathed nor shaved his beard, while none of the household women dared paint her eyes or dress her hair. Neferamon meanwhile was embalmed with the finest spices and wrapped in linen bands to the sound of whispered spells that none but the dead might hear. Blue and green rings were put on her fingers, amulets about her body, and at her neck a carved green scarab, engraved with a powerful prayer. Two coffins she had, one inside the other, each with her head upon it, showing her large dark eyes wide open and her mouth curved in an unaccustomed smile.

In this way she came home to us for her last procession, which was almost as lovely as if a daughter of Pharaoh were going to her grave. In front went the calf for the sacrifice, and the materials for feasting, the cakes, flowers, wine, and vases of perfume. Next came her own bed of ivory and gold, carved with the potbellied figure of the little god of sleep. We gave her chests of fine linen, armchairs, stools, and her toilet table, filled with eye paint and perfume. She had her great round earrings, fillets of jeweled flowers, and collars gleaming with bright enamel and gold. There were even little green glazed figures of servants to do her work in the land of the dead. Her feasts, her musicians, her palace, and her gardens were waiting, painted on the rock walls of her tomb for her spirit to enjoy. All the treasures of her life upon earth had been given to her spirit to delight in, as though there was anything there of which she had not wearied already.

None of the ceremonies that could honor her were wanting. There were hired mourners, repeating with parrot cries the conventional phrases. The high priest himself, girt with a leopard skin, was sprinkling the perfume. Oxen towed her shrine to the water. The beautiful death boat with its palms and lotus flowers received it there. On the shoulders of her nearest friends, it was borne into the western hills.

At the tomb the last farewells were spoken, the sacrifice was offered, and the feast consumed in honor of the dead.

The high priest by a spell released her from the bonds of her dead body to the strange and shadowy life which was now hers.

"Do not wear out your hearts with sorrow," sang the harpist, turning to us, "but be happy while you live. Your own life is short, and your lamentations do not benefit those who have gone."

We turned away and went home without my mistress. Much had been given her, but even so Penamon remembered that more might be needed in the long twilight of her eternity. Though she had feasts upon her walls, he sent her wine and meat. Though she had gardens, he gave her flowers. Though she had amulets and scrolls about her body, he offered prayers. Every new moon the priests brought these things to her chapel, that her soul might delight in them and be at peace. Surely never was a spirit granted more richness and more ease.

The valleys of the dead are not deserted. Scattered in the hollows of the hills lie villages of workmen, of priests who give the monthly offerings, and of watchmen who protect the dead from thieves. It was from these guards that a messenger came to Penamon about three moons later and was received by him in his hall of audience after he had dismissed his crowd of petitioners for that day.

The messenger was a priest, a little wizened man whose shaven head was leathery brown from long exposure to the sun. With many nervous bowings, he besought Penamon to inspect for himself the seals of Neferamon's tomb.

Penamon's face grew very grim. "If the tomb has been robbed within these few weeks, you rascals all will die for it," said he. "Both priests and guards alike."

The little man, who had raised himself to a standing pos-

ture with his hands respectfully in the air, now bobbed forward nervously again until his head was almost level with
his knees. "There has been no robbery," he protested in
quavering tones. "I swear that you will find every seal
intact."

"Why then inspect them?"

The priest hesitated. "Someone was seen," admitted he.
"It was only a white shape at a distance, but the tomb is well
known to be exceedingly rich."

"Take guards, then, and catch your prowler," retorted
Penamon with impatience. "Why trouble me with this
affair?"

"We have tried," said the little priest, "but we cannot draw
off patrols from elsewhere until we know what is the real
object of these thieves. We have taken no bribes in this
matter, O Penamon, but we are afraid of bearing the blame
if any harm is done."

Penamon put his chin on his hand and looked at him, considering a little. "If you were not honest, you would not
have come to me," he remarked. "I will send you extra
guards."

From that time three men were deputed to watch nightly
by the tomb of Neferamon, while the regular patrols went
up and down the valley as before. Until the time of the full
moon, nothing happened. Then, however, the little priest
appeared once more in Penamon's hall of audience, pushing
before him a gigantic Nubian, who cast himself face down
on the floor before my master, quivering with fright in every
limb.

Penamon signed to his fanbearers, for the day was hot.
"Well?" said he.

The priest seemed nervous also. "I have — " He licked

his lips. "I have brought this guard whose accent is less bar-
barous than that of the others, in order that you may hear
from his own lips what he has seen."

He poked the Nubian sharply with his foot until the latter
lifted his face an inch or two above the ground and cried, "It
was a woman, haggard and no longer young. She stood in
the moonlight by the tomb, clad in white and wearing a fillet
set with a great green stone!"

There was an instant's total silence. Even the fanbearers
paused in their work for a moment until Penamon signed to
them hastily. He turned to the Nubian. "How came this
woman to the tomb?" demanded he.

"She was there, and then she was not there. She stood
before the entrance, and we all saw her clearly in the light
of the moon."

"It is well. You may go." The Nubian raised himself
hastily to a crouching position and backed out from Penamon's presence, his eyes always on the floor. When he had
left, Penamon turned to the priest. "What devil possesses
Nefaramon that she cannot even rest among the dead?" said
he.

"No one who lives in those valleys," said the priest, regarding him seriously, "can find strange sights or sounds unnat-
ural amid so many dead. Sometimes when the spirit tires of
its twilight life, it will wander abroad, but it seldom ventures
very far."

"When the spirit tires!" repeated Penamon bitterly.
"What can satisfy such a woman? Will she never be still?"

"She has palaces and gardens in her tomb," the priest reminded him, "which are far more delightful than the desolate
valley outside. She will soon be wearied of that."

"She wearied of everything," said Penamon. "I would

give half my wealth if she would only burden me no more."

He sighed again and sat thinking, unaware no doubt that the tidings were already abroad in his household that the mistress walked again. By nightfall, every slave but myself had heard the story, and the girls were tittering in corners, vowing they would not walk across the courts alone.

It was one of the slave boys who made the first commotion as he was bringing in a jar of scented water for my master's bath. Suddenly he gave a loud scream and dropped the pitcher, so that the whole household came running to discover the source of the noise. "I saw her!" he yelled. "I saw her with the green stone in her hair!"

There was naturally an immense sensation. Every would-be heroine claimed to have seen a white garment whisk around a corner, to have heard a strange noise, or to have felt a sensation that had raised the very hair erect on her head. Even the cooks and stableboys, who had no business in the

master's quarters, were crowding in to increase the tumult until I made the surly old porter take a stick and disperse them. "The boy is hysterical," I declared to sober them, "and he deserves a good beating to teach him that spirits do not venture so far away from their tombs."

So I honestly thought until, the disturbance over, I made my way to the little recess where I slept in my mistress's room. Right inside the doorway I came upon her, close enough for me to have touched her if I had dared put out my hand. I looked full at her, and she at me. There was an awful silence in which I could hear the painful thudding of my heart. The room was dark, yet to all appearances she stood in moonlight, dressed in a brief, white robe such as poor women wear. I could see she had bracelets and rings, while about her head was a golden fillet set with a great green jewel. Well I knew this adornment, since I myself had taken it out and given it into the hands of those who had prepared Neferamon for death. Her lips moved, and on her face was such a weary expression of despair that my very heart was wrung.

It was as the Nubian had said. She was there, and then she was not there. She did not return, though I lay awake to watch for her until dawn.

Penamon was so angry when I told him of this visitation that he utterly refused to share my compassion for her. He was a hard man who worshiped justice and could feel no pity where he had condemned. Having done much more than his duty by my mistress, he blamed her ingratitude and would not willingly see or speak with her again. Instead, he went to the high priest and had a letter written which was left with the proper incantations in her tomb. "You have forgotten your duty," he reproved her, "though I have remembered mine. Leave me alone, lest I accuse you before the judgment seat of Osiris, god of the dead. Reflect what punishment will be yours when the god condemns you, as he must when he hears how fully your needs were satisfied."

Many a ghost would have been frightened away by such a letter, since there could be no doubt that Penamon's complaint was just. My mistress, however, braved his anger to come again nightly, appearing most often in her own chamber, yet frequently also in the corridor outside. No punishment would induce the slaves to render the simplest service to Penamon, or to appear on any pretext in the master's quarters after dark. I alone continued to meet her out of pity, for it seemed to me that she turned to us not in spite, but in despair.

Eight nights had passed since the writing of this letter before I could persuade Penamon to speak with her himself. I lighted the little lamp which I now always set by me, while he waited by the wall in his armchair, chin on hand. Nothing that I could say had softened him toward her. In the flickering lamplight, he might have been an image carved in the hardest, coldest stone.

She came about midnight, suddenly visible in that strange, moonlit radiance of her own. Of the two, it was the ghost who caught her breath with a little shudder, while Penamon stared at her coldly, showing not a trace of fear. "Leave us alone, Neferamon," he said to her with haughty command. "Have you not burdened us long enough with your restless ways?"

Tears gathered in her dark eyes at that, but they did not fall. We both could see that she sighed heavily. With a tremendous effort, she turned her head toward me and spoke.

"What do you want, my mistress?" cried I in desperation. "I cannot hear!"

"Your place is in the tomb," said Penamon brutally. "No one cares whether your spirit is happy there or not."

He spoke to empty air and darkness. Where my mistress had been, she was not any more. "If you did not encourage her, Nebtu," said Penamon harshly, "I do not think that she would want to return."

His severity angered me. "You are wrong!" cried I. "She will come back and back because her unhappiness is more than she can bear."

"She never bore it," retorted Penamon with bitterness. "Did I complain because she did not care for me?"

He spoke with more feeling than he was used to show, and I perceived for the first time that my master had been no happier than my mistress. He, however, had eaten out his heart in silence, while she had burdened us and him with her complaints. Perhaps it was natural that he resented being loaded with her sorrows as well as his own. He was a hard man to pity, but I felt a certain sympathy with him, though I dared not utter it. Instead, I looked away into the darkness and said quietly, "Did no one ever really care for her?"

"How should I know?" asked Penamon helplessly. "She was never happy with me."

"But her girlhood?" I persisted. "Was not that a happy time?"

Penamon's face grew very dark. "It was a good time for children because that accursed Pharaoh himself had a child-like heart. He lived in a fool's paradise where God was kind and everyone was loving, and he did not care that men starved in the rest of Egypt, and provinces were lost to vigorous enemies. The happiness of that time was like a poisoned flower."

Perhaps the darkness helped him to ease his bitterness with speech. We sat with the little light flickering between us, each turning away from the other into the shadows, as though we were speaking to ourselves. I questioned him gently. "What became of that lovely city where Pharaoh worshiped his kindly, foolish god?"

"It is deserted," he answered quietly. "Blown sand has choked the fountains, the gardens have withered, and even the palace that was so beautiful is returning to the dust. Egypt was crumbling when that Pharaoh died, and in their panic, men could not return to the old ways too fast. So hastily was the place abandoned that even the dogs were forgotten in their kennels, I have heard say. Only the palace children, who had been loved there and had seen no evil, wept when they left and hankered always after the past. None of them lived long, except Neferamon, and not one of them ever awakened from that enchanted dream."

I rose and felt my way across the room to the corner where the carved box of my mistress's jewelry was lying, empty of all but a few broken trinkets which had not been worth while placing in her tomb. There at the bottom I found the strange sign of the blessing sun and brought it to him. "Let her go back to her dream," said I, "since she is dead, and those times cannot harm Egypt any more."

"She kept it, then," said Penamon almost gently.

"She kept it," I agreed, "and I think she needs it now. If the dead are not content, a way lies open by which through strange perils they may journey toward the Islands of the Blessed. Each must have his talisman to protect him. This, I think, is hers."

"It cannot be!" said Penamon sharply. "Never can we let her go under the sign of such a god!"

"Let her depart," I answered him. "Have you not kept her long enough? All her life she has been waiting to go back into this dream. She may reach her goal, or she may perish. In any case, why should she linger here?"

Penamon took the golden sign and rose. "You are right, Nebtu," he said. "I will give her the talisman and let her set out whither she will. Is it not strange that so much sorrow should be so simply satisfied?"

He sighed as he went away. I sighed also, not for my mistress who went through strange ways after happiness, but for my master. In his conventional world there were no such expedients. He made the right gestures and said the correct words over the sacrifice. His god asked no more. Instead of happiness, he could only teach himself to have a heart of stone.

8

THE CHILDREN OF SET

A CERTAIN PHARAOH who was a great lover of magic had many wise men and miracle workers at all times in his court. Indeed, the day came when he had seen so many wonders that hardly anything could surprise him any more. His appetite for marvels, however, was not abated, and if he could not see a novelty, he desired to hear of one. When therefore a scribe presented a tale discovered on an ancient roll of papyrus, the king composed himself happily to listen, observing that people were more godlike in olden times and their powers more remarkable. With this encouragement, the scribe unrolled the top of his papyrus and thus began.

There was once a prince who had a fancy to travel about his dominions and passed through many villages where the peasants toiled from dawn to dusk for his sake. After several days, he reached the flowering pastures where his red and white cattle fed on the banks of great canals and marshy pools. Here as night fell, he came upon two herdsmen who had kindled a fire and were cooking outside a shelter which they had erected for themselves out of woven reeds. In the

red glaze they looked more like devils than men, unshaven
and with fierce eyes glittering beneath shaggy mats of hair.
The prince perceived that they had their crooks beside them,
the straight ends of which were shod with copper points like
spears. Being himself unarmed, he therefore thought it prudent to hide awhile and listen to them, that he might judge
what manner of men they were.

"It is better to run away and go for a soldier," grumbled
the nearest, taking his crook and giving an angry poke at the
fire. "I hardly dare go home at the end of the season without
more cattle. The prince is a cruel master, and his overseers
are always ready with the stick."

"That is so, indeed," agreed the second, who was a red-
haired youth with massive arms and chest as broad as a barrel.
"Nevertheless, why should you lose your cattle here? As it
seems to me, the grass never grew so thick about these parts
before."

"It is all very well for you, red-haired son of the demon
Set," retorted the first speaker. "No crocodile will touch a
red-haired man, for he fears the devil who protects him. I,
on the other hand, was born on a day over which those
beasts have special power."

"Where is this crocodile?"

"It waits by the ford that joins those two great pools,"
replied the first man gesturing. "Every day I must take my
cattle through the water there, and you may be sure that
there is no trick to protect them which I do not perform.
Having been born in an evil hour, I am careful to carry an
ibis feather, which should have power to turn the fiercest
crocodile to stone. I also know a strong spell that I always
say to the water. 'Halt, crocodile! Do not wave your tail or

move your legs. Do not open your mouth. May the water seem to you a barrier of fire. Halt, crocodile, son of the evil one!' "

"That is all good magic," nodded the red-haired man. "Do you mean to say that the crocodile is not turned to stone?"

"For seven days he was," admitted the other. "Though I could see his great snout in the water, he could not move as we went by. On the eighth day as I came down to the ford, I met a woman, a child of Set like yourself, with flaming hair and huge eyes the color of green pools. 'How dare you enchant my crocodile?' said she.

" 'Is he your crocodile?' asked I astonished, for even a red-haired one does not adopt such creatures.

" 'He is, indeed,' said she, 'and today we will wrestle a fall. Then if I win, the beast may have his pick out of your whole herd.'

" 'And if I win?' asked I, for she seemed both small and slender.

" 'Then I will teach you the magic of Thoth,' said she.

"With that I rushed forward to crush her in my arms, but she slipped sideways. How it was, I do not know, but I found myself traveling head over heels through the air. I came down with a splash in the water, and was lucky to do so, since if I had landed on dry ground, I should certainly have broken my neck. As I scrambled up, that crocodile slid past me, opening his mouth so close that I could have rammed my right hand down his throat. With a fearful snap, he closed on the finest bull in my herd, a great red yearling without so much as one white hair. As you may well suppose, the rest of them scattered in wild confusion, so that I have spent the whole of the day in rounding them up. This is all bad enough, but how shall I prevent this woman from levying tribute upon me on every occasion I must pass? What herdsman will be bold enough to wrestle with her for the magic of Thoth?"

"I will!" cried the prince, stepping forward into the firelight. "I can prevail, for I wear a talisman which I bought at a great price from the temple and which has hung round the neck of a god."

"Vanquish her if you can," said the red-haired man, looking up at him calmly. "But do not boast while the issue remains to be seen."

Very early the next morning, the herdsmen rounded up their cattle and took them down to the river, the prince going ahead with the young bulls, and the others following with the cows and calves. The ford was a wide, shallow stretch of water whose banks were trampled and muddy from the daily passing of the herd. In the cold light of the morning, it lay very quiet and still. It was not until the sun caught on a patch of water that the prince saw a woman, clad in a thin white garment and veiled in clouds of coppery hair.

"Good morning to you, prince of this land," said she. "Do

you think that the green stone at your breast gives you power
to wrestle such as I?"

"That and my own good courage," said the prince as he
laid his arms about her and crooked his leg behind her own.
For a moment the two swayed from side to side, panting,
while their bare feet made squelching noises in the mud.
"Admit my power!" said he through his teeth as he bent her
slowly backward, his cheek pressed hard against her own.

"It is great, but not enough," answered she. With that,
her arms went around him and began to squeeze his chest
like iron bands. Now she in her turn put a knee behind his
and bore him backward, but he clung to her so tightly that
she could not throw him down. Once more, therefore, he
said, "Admit my power!"

"Never!" cried she, and with a hand beneath his chin she
tore him from her and threw him full upon his back into the
mud.

Quick as a flash, the crocodile seized on the best milch cow
in the herd. The rest galloped panic-stricken out of the
water and fled lowing up the bank with the frantic herdsman
in pursuit.

"Now that is too much!" cried the red-haired man, and
with a roar he seized the woman and sent her whirling head
over heels into the stream.

She picked herself up, and the prince did likewise. They
turned to face each other, she waist-deep in the water, he
bespattered from head to foot with mud. "I should have conquered you!" cried he, shaking with anger. "But for this
clown here, I should have wrestled with you every day until
I won."

"We may meet again," responded she breathing heavily,

"but you will never learn from me the magic of Thoth."
With that, she smote upon the water with the palm of her
hand, and the crocodile came to her, pushing his broad snout
up the river like a great, gnarled log.

"Set your foot on his back," said she to the red-haired man,
"and take me by the hand." Side by side they stood on the
crocodile as he bore them across the water, and the risen sun
turned their flaming heads to gold. So brightly they flashed
that the startled prince blinked sharply. When he opened
his eyes again, they both were gone.

"So be it," said he shrugging his shoulders as he turned
away from the water. "I too know some magic and have
ways to find out more."

After this time, another fancy seized the prince. He began
to haunt the temples, endlessly deciphering the writings
carved on their talismans and on their walls. Day after day
he spent at the House of Life in Memphis, poring over
ancient scrolls from the library of the priests. It began to be
said that he was a magician and knew more secret wisdom
than any living man.

So matters stood when Pharaoh's only daughter lay on her
bed of carved cedarwood one night and could not sleep.
Then said a waiting woman who watched beside her, "Is it
fever which makes you turn, and sigh, and move your head-
rest up or down as though it did not fit you and was not
carved with many soporific spells?"

Pharaoh's daughter sighed again and answered, "My
father grows old and must give me a husband who may in
time be god and king over the land. Sometimes he talks of
marrying me to his scarred and one-eyed general. At other
times, he thinks of his wrinkled minister, or again of his

shaven, monkey-faced high priest. Now if I could but know which fate would come upon me, I might bear it. As it is, I have to dread not one, but three."

"It is not hard to read such things," replied the waiting woman. "Before the sun comes up, you must take a golden bowl, go barefoot into the meadows, and fill it to the brim with dew. Turn your face to the east and wait until the rising sun shines on the water. Then repeat the words that I shall teach you, look in the bowl, and you shall see the face of him you are to wed."

Very early on the next morning, when the mist was on the ground and the sky was not yet gray, Pharaoh's daughter took a bowl of gold and went out into the meadows of clover to gather dew. When the first rays of the sun shone on the water, she muttered the strange words her woman had told her, and glanced into the bowl. As soon, however, as she saw what lay within it, she gave a fearful shriek and collapsed on the grass as though she were dead. When her servants came running out to raise her, she opened her eyes, but could neither speak nor walk, and so she remained.

With one accord the whole band of the king's magicians declared that an evil demon had seized on the princess and must be expelled. They therefore surrounded her with balls of clay and spittle in which they had kneaded snakeskin, hairs from a sacred bull, roots dug by moonlight, and little amulets that had been laid upon a corpse. They lighted braziers and filled the gay chamber with the pungent smoke of herbs. They swayed and chanted, calling upon the aid of powerful gods. Daily the brow of the god and king appeared more anxious, while his minister, his priest, and his general whispered together, making common cause now that the princess was beyond the reach of all.

At last when Pharaoh saw that he had no help from his magicians, and that the very images from the temple had visited his daughter in vain, he sent swift boats up and down the river to the farthest parts of his kingdom, declaring that anyone who could cure the princess might have her to wife. Thus all the wise men of the kingdom flocked to the palace, with their staffs, their scrolls, and the paraphernalia of their magic, but even the oldest and most repulsive among the holy men of Egypt brought no cure.

As for the prince, he did not go with the others, but told Pharaoh's messengers, "There is only one magic that will cause the dumb to speak and the lame to walk. That is the magic of Thoth, and as I do not know it, I will not go to the daughter of Pharaoh until it is found. It does not lie in the temples, but in the marshlands, where once I met a woman who knew what it was." With these words, he called for his own boat, painted in blue and picked out with gilding, in which he went about his own dominions seated under a canopy of palms. He bade his rowers take him to the eastern arm of the Delta, and set him on shore where the grasslands and the marshlands both begin.

On this eastern side of the Delta lies a wide, flat country where thatched huts rise on little hillocks amid stagnant ponds or acres of whispering reeds. Flickering lights move across the marsh in the darkness at some seasons, and wise men do not travel at such times. During the day it is a noisy country, full of the sighing of winds and the screaming of birds. It is a land in which a man's cry goes unheard or unregarded, though men have disappeared in the mud from time to time. Even the fowlers keep to the slimy pools about their villages, while farther in, where the water is deep and dark green, they do not dare to go.

Through this country went the prince, walking first on
the high causeways that led through inhabited parts, and
then plunging across the mud on tracks known only to the
wildcats, snakes, or foxes that preyed upon the creatures of
the marsh. Birds hung about his head uttering cries of strange
omen. Snakes hissed, but seeing the green stone at his breast,
they slid away. The little marsh lights danced and flickered
around him, leading to bottomless tracts of quaking mud.

At last he came to the center of the marsh and saw that
within it there lay a dark lake, surrounding an island on
which grew thick, green bushes like a wall. He glanced at
the water, in which were neither weeds nor fishes, and saw,

uncoiling himself from the· depths, a water snake. The creature lifted his head from the surface and hissed as the prince passed by him, searching for a place where solid ground gave access to the water's edge. Presently he found a spot where the reeds grew thinly, and he halted, scanning the water before him carefully. A little red eye blinked at him and with a roar a great black hippopotamus opened his jaws so wide that the prince could see down his huge red mouth into his throat. The prince passed on once more and came to a little cove with a small, firm beach of sand. He looked across at the island and at the water in between. All was absolutely still. Advancing a single pace, he wetted his feet in the lake. With an imperceptible motion a great gray log came floating along the shore.

The prince regarded the log, and partway down its length he saw a cold, fishy eye that stared at him. Then he knew his search was at an end and said to himself, "Here is the giant crocodile, and with him must be the children of Set." With that, he took a small scroll from his bosom and struck the water, murmuring powerful words. With a great roar the lake divided before him, piling itself upon either side as though it had been contained by walls of glass. The prince set foot on the road which lay between them, leading straight as an arrow to the island in their midst.

A red-haired man came down to the bank of the island and stood there watching the prince as he walked across. "Why should I not pick you up and throw you head over heels into the water where my monsters could finish you off?" cried he.

The prince looked at him and saw that he was broad and burly as ever, and that his red beard still made a bush about his face. He was clothed no longer in rags, but in fine white linen, and a broad collar of gold lay round his neck. He raised his hands as though to seize on the prince, who smiled at him unconcerned and answered, "If I perish, you will never get rid of this path to your island. Give me what I ask, and I will show you how waters divide, and how they may be closed."

"What do you want?" said the magician, scowling. "There has been trouble between us both since the day when you tried to win the magic of Thoth instead of me."

"Give me a charm that can cure Pharaoh's daughter, and you shall have that which makes the waters divide."

"That is no fair exchange," said the magician, "but you shall have what you ask, and it will go hard if I cannot find means to make things even." Thereupon he brought out a box of iron and took from it another box made of cedar-wood and marked with mysterious carvings. In this was a box of ebony and ivory, containing another of silver, which in its turn when opened revealed a casket of gold. In the golden casket lay a small and tattered papyrus, yellow with age and marked with mysterious signs in a strange, black ink. This the magician plunged into a bowl of water, dabbing and pressing on it with his fingers until the ink was completely washed away. Then he poured the blackened water into a vial and gave it to the prince, saying, "This has the power of the words which were written on the papyrus. Let the princess take three sips, and she will be cured. I warn you, however, you had best not think to marry her, for it is not her destiny."

"I think it is," answered the prince, "but that is a matter which you and I must settle on some different ground. Meantime, do you walk back with me through the water, and I will give you my charm when I am safe on the farther bank."

After some days, the prince came up to Pharaoh's city in his blue and gold barge, while all the people flocked to the wharf to stare at it. The princess still lay on her cedarwood couch in the palace with charms heaped all about her, consisting of clay images, rolls of papyrus, carvings, stones, pieces of skeletons, or strange dried skins. Sweet and pungent smokes poured from a number of braziers. Naked black men, bearded Syrians, red-eyed enthusiasts, priests, and ragged beggars howled or whirled before her, some after the fashion of their country even gashing themselves with knives.

"Turn all this trash out!" commanded the prince. With relief the servants began to gather up the charms in armfuls and throw them into the yard. With howls of protest, the wise men ran after them to rummage, each for his own treasure, in the heaps outside.

"Bring fans to drive away this smoke," ordered the prince, "and clean the chamber." He waited in silence, leaning against one of the painted pillars while this was done.

At last the chamber was swept clean and strewn with silvery sand in which was mingled the dust of lapis lazuli. Fresh lotus garlands were hung upon the pillars, that their scent might purify the air. The prince called for a cup and, filling it from his vial, he lifted the princess slightly in order that she might drink.

At the first sip, the princess sat up and looked about her, so that the servants cried out and ran to Pharaoh with the news. "There is more to do yet," said the prince as he held the draught to her lips the second time.

At the second sip, the princess stood and walked, but though she turned her eyes from one to another and opened her mouth, no utterance came. When the prince offered

her the cup for the third time, she took it in her own hands
and drank from it. With a sudden gesture she turned aside
to her waiting woman and said, "It is not he." Bursting into
a passion of weeping, she hid her face upon the woman's
neck.

At this moment appeared the god and king, almost running and with his fanbearers stumbling beside him in a panting effort to keep up his dignity. With infinite relief he
welcomed the prince, having long repented his rash promise,
since he had seen what sort of folk had flocked to the palace
with their nasty cures. "Of all the princes in my dominions,"
said he rejoicing, "this one is the fittest to be god and king
over Egypt after me."

Meanwhile the princess went on weeping and said to her
woman, "If it were only he!"

Great were the preparations for the princess's wedding,
but she took no part in them except to send to the temples
and ask if he who had cured her should indeed have her to
wife. The images with one accord nodded their heads to
this question, as much as to say in full sight of the priests and
people, "It shall be he."

"It was not his face that I saw in the golden bowl," said
the princess to her woman. "How then can the gods themselves declare that I must marry him?"

"You are to marry the man who truly cured you," replied
the green-eyed waiting woman, "that is, not he who gave
you the draught, but he who owned the spell. How do we
know that this prince is a true magician and has not stolen
the charm from someone greater?"

"But how shall I find this out?" asked the princess trembling.

"I will teach you," said the waiting woman. She brought

out a talisman shaped like a fish and carved of smooth green malachite, which she hung about the princess's neck, while instructing her in what she should do and say.

In the last hours of the day when Pharaoh visited his house of women, the princess went to him, saying, "Though you have given me a lake for my own pleasure and set a golden boat on it which shines like the sun, you have never yet joined me there in the cool of the evening, to hear the sound of soft singing across the water as my women row about."

This suggestion pleased the Pharaoh, who was tired of his draughtboard and of the tales of ancient magic with which the women diverted him. He went down to the golden boat, which the princess had caused to be strewn with scarlet cushions that she and her father might lie at their ease beneath the canopy, instead of sitting stiffly side by side in chairs. They therefore lay on the deck and listened to the women singing, while the princess dabbled her arm in the water, leaning out across the side. As they reached the center of the lake, the fish of green malachite which the princess was wearing dropped off her neck and vanished with a little plop into the depths beneath.

The princess began to weep and wail, "My fish! My fish of green malachite! Without this jewel all my luck has gone from me!"

Then said the waiting woman from her place among the rowers, "Is not the prince a great magician? Could he not recover your malachite fish from the very bottom of the sea?"

The princess appeared comforted at this saying, while Pharaoh himself nodded his head as he declared, "There is much sense in this waiting woman. Though she has green

eyes like a daughter of Set, her appearance is almost pleasing
when one considers the wisdom of her words." He therefore sent for the prince and bade him fetch the fish of green
malachite, adding that it should be but a very small matter
to raise such a jewel, even from the depths of the sea.

The prince looked at the bright water and shook his head,
declaring that he was not magician enough to recover the
talisman. Even Pharaoh frowned at that, while the princess
turned from him passionately, crying, "If that be the case,
you are not magician enough for me!" To this she adhered,
notwithstanding all entreaties; and she worked upon her
father until he too became angry, not having been used to
demand a service which was not performed. Before the sun
was set, there was a quarrel in the palace and the promised
hand of the princess was now refused.

On the following morning, the prince went down to the
wharf, thinking to summon his rowers and depart the way
he had come. As he reached it, he was aware that crowds
of citizens had gathered to stare at a boat which was approaching up the stream. Unlike most rich men's boats, this
was not gilded or painted in bright colors, but appeared a
plain dark gray from stem to stern. This in itself was unusual, but what was extraordinary was that the rowers
themselves were from head to foot a plain dark gray. They
were not yellowish, like Syrians, brown like Egyptians, or
any of the shades of black which Ethiopians display, but
were gray in their skins and their hair and what could be
seen of their costume, all alike. Indeed, except on their passenger, there was no color visible but darkish gray.

In his chair of state under a gray awning sat a huge brown
man clad in white and wearing a golden collar. Before his
flaming head and bristling countenance, the harmless citizens

shrank back in mild dismay, leaving a little space by the
landing into which the stranger stepped without a word.
Turning to his gray boat, he picked it up, whereupon it
dwindled in his hand and shrank into a tiny model of gray
wax. Muffling it in his robe, he turned himself about, de-

manding, "Where is the palace of the Pharaoh, whose
daughter my servant cured for me?"

No one dared answer him, but the people made a lane
down which he stalked, head high and with the little gray
boat beneath his arm. It chanced that Pharaoh was in his
hall of audience, wearing the red and white crown and receiving the tribute which kings had sent to him from the
ends of the earth. If a god may be said to turn pale, then
this one did so when his eyes fell on the fiery countenance of
the son of the evil one. His crook and his scepter shook in

his hands as he demanded in quavering tones, "How dare
this son of the devil face my good godhead on my golden
throne?"

"I have come for your daughter," answered the evil one
in ringing tones, "your only daughter, whom I sent my servant to cure, and whom you have promised to give me as
wife."

The god and king shivered again, for he was old and the
courage of his youth had long forsaken him. His wizened
minister leaned forward and said to him with soft malice,
"Would it not be well to ask the princess what she says?"
Thereupon the one-eyed general and the monkey-faced
priest nodded agreement, making common cause in their
jealousy against the prince.

The princess gave a little cry when her eyes fell on the
red magician. She went pale as ashes to her very lips, but
she did not faint or run away. "I cannot tell who cured me,"
she admitted, "but I did see this terrible face in my golden
bowl."

Now the Pharaoh looked on the red man, dismayed and
silent, for this was worse than giving his daughter to one of
the madmen who gashed themselves with knives. In his
extremity, a thought came to him, and he said, "In that case,
you can recover us the fish of green malachite that lies at
the bottom of the lake."

"Gladly," said the magician, and he strode off through
the palace followed by the minister, the priest, the general,
and even the Pharaoh with his stumbling fanbearers half
running in his wake. At the edge of the lake, the red man
took out a scroll, bent down, and struck the water, muttering at the same time some magic words. With a roar, the
waters divided, piling themselves up on either side as though

they had been contained by walls of glass. The magician turned to the wizened minister, who stood quaking beside him. "Walk in and fetch the fish of malachite. You will not need to wet your foot," said he.

With a groan, the little old minister tottered forward, giving many an anxious glance at the water on either hand as he went staggering down the narrow lane. He picked up the fish and came hobbling back with all possible speed, while the magician grinned at his terror and the whole court stood amazed.

"Now shall I have the princess?" cried the evil one, taking the fish and tossing it to her, as he restored the lake with a roar of waters to its former state.

Once more the city hummed with preparations for a wedding, while the princess sat silent in her chamber, and even the waiting woman could get no smile from her. Days passed, and the feast was at last ready. By the hideous groom sat the princess, clad in her richest adornments, though in spite of her eye paint and lip salve, she looked pale as any ghost. The wine was being poured when there came a stir at the door, and a messenger went over to Pharaoh. "Here is the prince," he announced, "who is appearing to claim his bride."

In came the prince dressed like a bridegroom and demanded his wife before them all.

The Pharaoh looked from one bridegroom to the other, and though he knew which one he preferred, he did not dare to make a choice. "The princess has sat at her wedding by the man she saw in her golden bowl. Now turn him out, since he has served his purpose, and finish the feast with the true bridegroom," said the prince.

With a little cackle the wizened minister leaned forward

in his place. "At every feast there is some entertainment," he said, "and at this there should be one of a quite unusual sort. Let these two magicians show their powers before us, and let the stronger have the princess as bride. Many a tale will be told of this wedding in the days that lie ahead." He tittered a little with the general, who sat beside him, each hoping that both their rivals would be destroyed.

The red-haired man arose, nothing loath, and called to the servants to bring him in a goose. Chopping off its head, he placed this on one side of the hall, and threw the body over to the other. Then he made some magical passes, muttered some words, and behold, the goose came together and began to quack loudly and to peck with its beak at the crumbs on the floor.

"That is nothing," declared the prince, and he called for the attendants to bring him a bull. In his turn, he chopped off the head and disposed of the pieces on either side of the room. Then he made some magical passes, muttered some words, and the bull came together and stood in the midst of the room, snorting and snuffling, while the halter, which had fallen from his severed neck, still lay upon the floor.

Now when the red-haired one saw that his deed had been surpassed in this fashion, he gave a cry and sprang up where he stood in the form of a blazing fire. With shrieks the company parted on either side, and all fled into the courtyard, where the fire pursued them, catching at pillars and tables as it passed. Suddenly, there was a roar of thunder in heaven, and a great black cloud burst over them, drowning hall, pillars, and courtyard in a fierce downpour. In a moment the fire had been extinguished, the cloud had vanished, and the two magicians were facing each other in front of the dripping guests and blackened hall.

Once again with a shout the red one changed his shape and became a damp and clinging mist, which covered the palace in darkness and blotted out the kindly rays of the warming sun. With another great roar, a storm of wind fell on it and sent it flying with the wigs and garlands of the company bowling after it.

With a shriek the princess pointed to her waiting woman, whose heavy wig of ceremony had gone helter-skelter with the rest. All turned and saw that underneath it, her own hair was red as the magician's own. "Seize her!" cried the prince to those about her. "It is the daughter of Set."

When the red man saw that his accomplice was discovered, he determined to crush them all and changed himself into a falling roof of stone. But the boats of the sun and moon themselves came sailing down through the heavens, caught up the roof of stone, and bore it away. As for the waiting woman, when she saw the sun and the moon themselves were arrayed against her, she flew into the air like a great brown bird and disappeared. The sky was clear once more, and all was still. The prince looked around at the blackened ruins of the banquet, at the crownless Pharaoh and his wigless minister, and he gave his hand to the princess to lead her away. "Come with me," he said, "and we will hold a feast in my own palace whose richness will put the very banquet of Pharaoh to shame."

With that he led her toward the gate, while Pharaoh, hastily adjusting his crown, came tottering after. As for his fanbearers, they stayed behind, because the wind had left them nothing with which to sustain his dignity.

When the scribe had finished this tale, he paused. Pharaoh gave a long sigh of pleasure. "Those were the days of real marvels," he declared. "Miraculous cures I have seen, and miraculous plagues of wind, fire, pestilence, or rain, as the case may be. I have even beheld a conjuring trick like that with the bull and the goose. Waxen images, too, are common among us, though seldom on such a large scale as a boat and its rowers. As for the dividing of the waters, however, I do not believe that men could do such a thing in these modern days. I would give my very life to see that sight!"

A servant came into the hall and fell on his face before Pharaoh. "There is a man called Moses who declares that a spirit has bid him appear before your majesty."

"A miracle worker," cried the king, "since he talks of a spirit! Let him come in and show his powers, but such a thing as the dividing of water is not to be expected in our times."

9

THE LITTLE PHARAOH

IN FRONT of the blue gates of the palace garden, a small crowd of spectators lazily awaited the moment when Pharaoh would issue in splendor, as his daily custom was. Inside, the stable servants had already harnessed a pair of white horses to Pharaoh's light chariot, which shone with beaten gold. They had strapped gay plumes on the horses' heads, and were pulling back their arched necks with a tight bearing rein. The head slave of the stables in person was seeing to this, lest the little arms of the Pharaoh have trouble in restraining his spirited horses in the sight of the crowd.

In an open space inside the gate, lightly clad runners stood ready to dash panting through the streets before Pharaoh's chariot, and warn stragglers to stand out of his path. Twenty soldiers and fanbearers were approaching under the command of an officer from the quarters of the guards. Hor, the handsomest of the grooms, who had been chosen on that account to hold the heads of Pharaoh's horses, had taken up his position behind the runners, his hair smoothed over his ears, his body clad in a fresh white plaited kilt.

The golden chariot was led out, squeaking a little. Hor put up one hand to the bridle of the nearest horse, and the well-trained beasts stood still, while the chariots of the little queen and of the great lords began to range themselves in line.

There was a movement in the avenue from the palace. Hor stood like a statue as a pair of crouching fanbearers approached backward into his range of vision. Behind them, he knew, walked the Pharaoh, Tut-ankh-amon, girt with the magic jackal's tail and wearing his flashing apron of gold and enamel. Between the swaying fans, he could catch glimpses of the high white crown on the little head, its tip hardly reaching above the shoulder of Ai, the Master of Ceremonies, stalking behind him.

"This might be a great moment for me," thought Hor, as he always did. "God on earth, the child of Amon himself walks toward me while I hold his horses. He sees me."

There should have been excitement in this thought, but after two years there was none. Tut-ankh-amon would climb impassively into his chariot. The gates would open. Hor would stand aside, and the procession would dash out into the street. That would be all.

"And Ai will not see me," added Hor to himself. "Ai never sees me at all."

It was not to be expected that a very great prince like Ai, who was the keeper of the wealth of the kingdom, and who walked behind Pharaoh, should spare a glance for a handsome stable groom who happened to stand in his path. In the last two years he had never done so, and yet Hor had never completely given up hoping that he would.

On the day when Hor had first been promoted to stand by the horses of the god, he had made a visit to a certain red-

eyed fortuneteller, whose price was known to be a cheap
one because his sight was almost too dim to read the future
any more. Still, he was a good magician in his way and
knew powerful spells to recite as the sand trickled from his
fingers onto the ground. Almost immediately he had agreed
with Hor that by this recent promotion his fortune would
certainly be made.

"But whether it be good fortune or bad," he added dream-
ily, blinking at the sand with his head bent over until his
nose was almost touching it, "I cannot perfectly see."

"I have paid you a good silver bangle which one of our
mistress's women lost in the garden," said Hor indignantly.
"I have a good mind to take it back from you and break
your head."

"A truly lucky man reverences Mysteries," replied the
fortuneteller hastily, "and in any case there is more in the
sand." He put his nose down again to explore.

"Well?" urged Hor after the fortuneteller had smelled
over the ground in silence for a minute or two.

"A man with a cast in his eye," said he in puzzled tones
and without straightening up. "A very great man indeed."

"What about him?"

"In the right eye."

"Well, what has a very great man with a cast in the right
eye to do with me?" persisted Hor. "Will he be good for
me or bad?"

The fortuneteller sat up with a sudden jerk and began to
rub his eyes and whine. "What have I to do with princes?"
he complained. "A poor old blind man like me, and for the
price of an old copper bracelet washed over with silver!
How should I know that the very great man has anything to
do with you at all?"

"You old fraud!" shouted Hor, seizing him by the scruff of the neck. "So you were not too blind to see the bracelet was copper, but cannot read a man's fortune lying plainly before you! Get down on the ground and look more closely at it!" He tightened his grasp and rubbed the old man's nose in the sand.

Hor went home in a rage, but the very next day when he stood for the first time beside Pharaoh's horses and watched the fanbearers back down the avenue, with the top of the white crown appearing between their crouching forms, he became conscious that the prince behind Pharaoh squinted a little in one eye.

It was not a great deal of a cast, and after two years of watching, Hor could not always be sure it was there. Ai's eyes were deep-set, and he used no blue eye-shadow, as the other great lords did. Moreover his thin, lined face was always overhung by the curls of a monstrous wig, very thick at the sides and over the brow. On some days the wig was brown, sometimes it was blue, black, or even dusted with silver, but always it was encircled with a jeweled band. Wig and jewels together served to distract attention from the cautious face, as did the wide collar beneath it, flashing with enamel and precious stones.

Pharaoh put a small hand on the chariot rail and hoisted himself slowly in. The runners crouched with their hands on the ground in readiness for the start. Hor stood like a stone. The little queen had already mounted, while the lords and princes were taking their places behind. At this instant Ai, Master of Ceremonies, halted, one thoughtful eye measuring Pharaoh, who stood doll-like in the golden chariot. His glance slid slowly over the horses' backs and came to rest on Hor.

For a long moment Ai deliberately took in Hor from head to foot with a quiet and faintly questioning gaze. Hor dared not stir, but a slow red flush crept up under the fair skin he had inherited from his mother, a blue-eyed slave from the western islands of the sea. "Ai sees me!" he thought wildly to himself. "Fame and fortune are between the hands of Ai for a daring man to grasp." He stiffened with anticipation of he knew not what as the great man turned away.

The procession was ranged in order now, and Pharaoh raised his jeweled whip. Upon the sign, slaves flung back the heavy gates, and the runners dashed panting into the road. Hor sprang away from the horses, as Pharaoh, leaning forward, shook the reins.

The horses gathered their muscles together for a leap into the gateway, when the left-hand one suddenly raised a whinnying scream and reared back, appearing to go mad.

Afterwards it was found that thorns had been inserted under his harness in such a way that the slightest move would drive them deeply into the skin. The brute reared into the air, kicking out with his forehoofs, and fell upon his partner. He in his struggles to be loose broke his tight rein, put his head down, and bolted for the gateway, dragging the raging left-hand beast along.

The little queen gave a shriek as she saw the golden chariot bounce in the air and come down with a shattering crash. The white crown tumbled from Pharaoh's head, its jeweled streamers flying, and with it fell his majesty. In a second he was only a frightened little boy clinging for dear life to the chariot rail.

In an instant of time the horses were under the gateway. The chariot rocked within a handsbreadth of the vast square tower by the left of the entrance, swayed perilously a moment, and whipped back with fearful force against the tower on the right.

The queen screamed again and covered her eyes. She heard a splintering crash as the chariot hit the wall, and then a sound of galloping hoofs and yells outside. Against her will she peered through her fingers. The chariot itself lay in fragments at the foot of the tower, but in the middle of the entrance two dusty figures were rolling in a tangled heap on the ground.

Hor had been nearest to the Pharaoh as the horses made their desperate leap toward the gate. Moreover he had been tense with excitement, alert to seize whatever possible chance of service Ai had foreseen. In the instant that the rocking chariot swayed by the left-hand tower, he had jumped aboard, seizing Pharaoh around the waist. It had taken him a moment, however, to detach the child's frenzied

grip from the rail, with the result that the two shot out of
the chariot like stones from a sling only about half a second
before the final crash.

They hit the ground in a huddle, and the next instant was
all bumps and bruises, and someone else's knee in one's
mouth. As they came to rest in the roadway, people dashed
forward, while the little Pharaoh, who was first to get back
his breath, began to kick and scream like one possessed.

"My majesty is hurt! My sacred majesty is bleeding!
Leave my majesty alone!"

None of the attendants dared touch him, and Hor, who
was getting most of the kicks, made shift to scramble painfully to one side. The little Pharaoh got to his feet and came
after him. "Take that!" he cried furiously, landing a kick.
"Take that and that! My majesty is sore!"

A firm hand clamped tight on Pharaoh's shoulder and
pulled him away. "Your majesty is alive," said Ai smoothly.
"Thanks be to Divine Amon, your father, since if your godhead had taken flight this day, we should be left desolate on
earth."

"Let me go!" cried the little Pharaoh passionately. "I
very well know you would like to be son of Amon on earth
in my stead."

Ai dropped his hand at once and bowed slowly and
solemnly to Pharaoh. "Your majesty is angered," he answered as he straightened up, "but when the godhead is
himself again, he will remember that he cannot do without
Ai, his faithful servant, in whose hands all things in the kingdom are."

It was smoothly said, but there was a certain menace in the
politeness of Ai's tone which did not seem to escape the little
Pharaoh's ears. His eyes fell to the ground, and he scrabbled

moodily in the dust with his toe. The little queen deftly interposed herself between them.

"You are bruised, Lord of the Earth, and your dress is torn," she said gently to her husband. "Let my servants bathe and anoint you while a message goes to Amon, your father god, that he may excuse your visit to his temple this day. Give the brave servant some token, for truly he has preserved the happiness of us all."

Pharaoh took off a bracelet of gold and flung it on the ground beside Ai. "Do you reward the slave, Ai, my servant," he said sulkily, "since you love my majesty so well. It is not fitting that the lips of god should be opened to such a one as he."

Hor stood before Ai, body bent forward in an attitude of reverence until his hands swung level with his knees. There was silence except for the shuffling feet of the departing procession, while Ai once more looked him up and down. "Pick up your bracelet, slave," said Ai calmly. "To deserve the favor of Pharaoh is not to earn it, but I will see that you are promoted to something fitting by and by."

Hor stood still humbly, not daring to look up until Ai had turned away. Then stooping rapidly for the bracelet, he cast a glance at the great man's retreating form.

"Something fitting!" he said to himself. "Ai's voice was very cool toward me, as though I had far from earned his favor by saving Pharaoh's life. It is all very well to have attracted the great man's notice, but I begin to wonder whether I should not have beaten the truth out of that fortuneteller, come what might."

After this incident, certain slaves mysteriously disappeared from the stable, and one of the great lords was appointed to inspect the harness of Pharaoh every day. Apart from this, events went on as before for nearly a whole moon. At the end of this time the head slave of the stable, a sour old man with a jealous eye for those in favor, sent for Hor.

"Perhaps I should not have ventured to take up the time of the savior of the All-Highest," he remarked with venom as the young man presented himself.

"We were cleaning the stables, and I stopped only to wash myself, lest I appear unmindful of the honor of your notice," answered Hor hastily. "We born slaves do not forget that until the Syrian Rebellion you were a free man with horses and slaves of your own."

"Very proper! Very proper!" nodded the head slave much gratified. "To be sure my position is somewhat different, and our masters notice it. It is a delicate attention on the part of a great prince like Ai that his orders to the grooms of the stable go through me. A distinguished man knows where to condescend!"

Hor's heart beat faster, but he had learned in a hard school not to show eagerness. "It is hardly probable that Ai would give a thought to a miserable groom without your recommendation," he suggested.

"Very true! My recommendation!" The old man was delighted. "He is an honest lad," I said to Ai, "and knows his station. Promotion will not go to his head. The upshot is that you are to ride in the chariot with Pharaoh when he goes into the hills to shoot gazelle. Pharaoh will drive himself, you understand, but you are to stand behind him and hold the reins also, as the god has not yet come to his full strength. There has been some talk about the accident at the gateway, and the lord who stands behind Pharaoh's throne is naturally the target for every base suspicion."

"I suppose," said Hor carefully, "that if there were a

second accident up in the hills and the wretched slave were killed with Pharaoh, no blame at all could attach to Ai, who had placed a servant of such tried faithfulness in his master's chariot."

"Just so!" the old man nodded with pleasure. "You have indeed a quick perception. If the wretched slave were killed with Pharaoh! What an honor! But of course the god hunts only gazelle and antelope, harmless creatures. In the Great King's day there were hundreds of lions in the passes of the hills, literally hundreds. He used to slay them singlehanded and in such vast numbers that if you wanted a lion now, you would have to fetch him clear over the desert from the wretched lands of the Libyans, which is hardly possible. You are to inspect the harness for yourself and choose the horses; in fact Ai has put the young god's life completely into your hand."

"He has indeed," sighed Hor reflecting. "There is a certain old fortuneteller who is dead now, but whom I should have beaten soundly while I had the chance."

On the afternoon of the third day when the heat was past, Pharaoh went hunting. It immediately appeared that he wished to stand alone in his chariot as the grown men did, and he was sulkily determined to make things difficult for Hor. He would deliberately jerk himself about at every bump, and Hor would have to dodge him, lest the sacred person of the god be offended by the common touch of a slave. Since the chariot was very small, open at the back, and entirely springless, it seemed probable that long before the hills were reached, Hor would be lying flat on his back in the road. Such was evidently the Pharaoh's intention, and to make matters worse, the horses of Ai followed so

closely that Hor would hardly avoid being trampled if he
fell to the ground.

For the first few miles of that journey the lords and attendants were openly grinning at the scene ahead of them in
Pharaoh's chariot, but Hor was too busy to notice or mind.
He was hopping frantically from one side to the other, or
leaning out over the back, one hand on the reins, which he
dared not pull, and the other grabbing for dear life at the
rail. Fortunately Pharaoh himself was improving in humor
as the gasps and thumps of his unhappy servant made music
in his ears. There was a faint suspicion of a smile on his face,
and he began to relax, the more especially as the path they
were traversing was now leaving the fertile green fields by
the river and pushing out into the western desert land,
strewn with sand and occasional boulders. Here it was
necessary for Pharaoh to concentrate on driving if he wished
to show the lords behind that he was master of his chariot.
He took a firmer grip of the reins and bent forward over
the rail. Behind him, Hor carefully suppressed a sigh of
relief.

The high plateau of the western desert came tumbling
down into the Valley of the Nile in an irregular cascade of
rocks which was split by narrow, twisting valleys where occasional springs nourished some vegetation. At the mouth
of one of these gullies waited the huntsmen with their pack
of hyena-like dogs, wolf dogs, and greyhounds, all straining
at the leash. For twenty-four hours at least these men and
their attendant beaters must have been driving game into the
head of this valley in order that Pharaoh and his lords
might have good sport. Already the sun was far down
the sky, and fantastic shadows mingled with bars of rose-

gold light to make strange patchwork on the jagged rocks. It was the cool hour when wild creatures came out of their shelters to refresh themselves at such little pools as the valleys possessed.

"We have beaters posted in the hills around," the chief of the hunters said. "My men declare that great flocks of gazelle and antelope have been driven into this pass."

"Let the dogs loose," commanded Pharaoh. "My majesty will go forward." He suited the action to the word as the dogs tore into the narrow, winding paths up the sides of the gully, followed by the huntsmen armed with long sticks and filling the echoes with halloos.

There was a little pool around a bend of this valley, not deep, but already dark with the shadows of evening. Beside it Pharaoh stopped his chariot, took the reins from Hor, and tied them about his waist, so that he might with a bend of his body direct the horses. He took an arrow from his quiver and fitted it carefully to his light bow of polished horn. Hor, left with nothing to do, glanced quickly around

him and saw that the nobles were preparing to lasso their game
with long straps weighted with stones at one end, leaving the
shooting entirely to the king. The black fanbearers and the
soldiers of the escort, though chosen for their speed and
endurance, came thankfully to a halt behind Pharaoh, panting heavily. Swarms of flies, scenting perspiration, buzzed
around them savagely. Hor laid a cautious hand on the
hunting spear which stood by Pharaoh's quiver and tested it
to see that it slipped easily out.

Little pebbles were falling down the rocky hillsides, while
the rattle of sticks and the cries of the invisible beaters were
beginning to be mingled with the patter of galloping feet.
A hare came bounding through the rough sagebrush of the
valley, swerved suddenly, and vanished into the shadow of
the rocks. Another followed and another, but the little
Pharaoh, paying no attention to such game, stood with his
bow at full stretch, unwilling to waste his first unhurried
shot on an inferior quarry.

A frightened ibex came dashing headlong down the sides
of the rock, only to draw up short as he became aware of
the danger ahead. For an instant he hesitated, and in that
moment the bow twanged. The little Pharaoh, allowing
for the probable direction of his swerve with the true instinct of a marksman, dropped him head over heels with an
arrow in his chest.

Hor's heart bounded with admiration at that first, splen-
did shot, though he modestly left it to the lords and attendants to break into cries of applause. In another few moments the whole valley was a wild confusion of mountain
sheep, gazelle, antelope, jackals, and smaller creatures. The
Pharaoh, who could not yet control himself amid excitement, began shooting so much at random that Hor perceived

the reason for all the company being posted so very respectfully behind. His arrows glanced off rocks in every
direction; they whizzed over the ears of the patient horses;
they even stuck in the ground a few feet from the chariot
itself. Now and then one hit some animal or other, at which
the Pharaoh raised a yell of pleasure and jumped for joy,
with the result that his next shot went anywhere.

The first rush of the frightened animals was quickly over.
A few stragglers appearing around the bend of the ravine
saw the confusion ahead and dodged back into safety, pre-
ferring to try to outwit the beaters along the rocky trails.
Before Hor had time to make any movement, the Pharaoh
suddenly loosened the reins by leaning forward while he
slashed savagely at the horses with his bow. The soldiers of
the escort had not time to do more than raise their shields
and straighten before Pharaoh had vanished up the little
ravine in a cloud of dust.

Taken off balance by the sudden move, Hor grabbed
fiercely at the rail once more and narrowly escaped being
thrown out on the ground headlong. With a shattering
crash the chariot hit a stone as it rounded a corner. It
bounded high in the air, coming down with such violence
that nothing but its beautiful workmanship saved it from
breaking apart. Careless for once of knocking against his
royal master, Hor put his arms around Pharaoh's body and
seized the reins, leaning backward and pulling with all his
strength. To his relief, the well-trained horses immediately
responded, coming violently to a halt in a small, almost cir-
cular space between jagged rocks. For the moment this was
empty of beaters, though they were to be heard farther up
the pass and could be glimpsed on the hillsides far above

their heads. Neither sheep nor antelope were to be seen. The only animal visible anywhere was a lion.

The creature was standing on a low rock in full view, half turned away from them toward the head of the valley where shouts and barking were coming very close. Hor had scant time for wondering how the lion had got there before Pharaoh, tearing himself free from his slave's embrace, let fly an arrow that hit the beast directly in the ribs at point-blank range.

It was a good shot, though appallingly foolhardy, since Pharaoh's thin arms, which could not control his horses, drew far too light a bow to kill a lion. With a terrible roar, the animal turned upon them. As it sprang Hor hurled the hunting spear and hit it full on the wicked head protected by the heavy skull and matted hair. He did nothing but divert the beast a little, yet only this and the panic of the horses saved them. Each of the horses strove to turn the opposite way and reared in a maddened effort to force his brother round. Thus the lion's spring, which had been shortened by Hor's attack, fell full upon the horses, encumbered as they were by their harness and the chariot pole.

Hor had not waited to see the effect of his weapon, but leaped for his life from the rocking chariot, dragging Pharaoh helplessly after him. They rolled behind a rock, just clear of the terrible struggle in which the chariot swung around and was shattered, the horses kicked savagely, and the growls and screams of the fighting animals rose on the air. Staggering to his feet, Hor saw the left-hand horse tear itself free and gallop off, streaming with blood from various gashes. The other was down on the ground and struggling, but feebly. There was no time to be lost. Hor snatched at the Pharaoh's bow, which lay beside him, but the arrows were strewn in the wreck of the chariot a little way off. Desperately he ran in and tried to seize one, but the movement merely attracted the attention of the raging beast. Turning from the dying horse, it struck out viciously at Hor and felled him with a great, raking blow from its front paws. Even as it did so, the frantic soldiers of the escort burst into sight around the rock and discharged an irregular volley of spears.

Diverted from Hor by these new tormentors, the lion gathered himself together and tried to spring. Evidently he could not, for his sides were bristling with spears, and for an instant he collapsed upon the ground. Then raising himself upon his forelegs, he began to crawl forward, roaring terribly and with the evident intention of killing once more before he died. So formidable was his appearance that the soldiers scattered before him, most of them having already thrown their hunting spears. For a moment the narrow bend was a scene of confusion, as the fleeing soldiers collided with the lords and the huntsmen coming up after them.

Fortunately for some, the lion's strength was exhausted. He could go no farther, but stood there roaring at them until the cliffs re-echoed, supporting himself upon his forepaws, and with four spears sticking in his side. One man, bolder than the rest, ran in with a sword to make an end. Before he could do so, the animal fell with one last defiant roar. Men rushed past him hastily to assist the Pharaoh, who had picked himself up and was regarding a little shakily the ruin he had caused.

Hor, who had not completely lost consciousness, was vaguely aware of the little Pharaoh crying, "He is my first lion. I hit him! I am going to be a lion hunter like my great-great-grandfather. You must measure him from head to tail at once!" Hor groaned feebly, and a man knelt by him with a water skin. He unstoppered the pipe and let it run a little, but Hor could not raise his head to drink. He groaned again.

Servants came over to fan away flies and to try and bandage Hor's chest with such pieces of their garments as they could spare. "He ran in on the lion," said the captain of the soldiers. "Had it not been for him, the beast would have sprung upon Pharaoh."

"Will the man die?" asked the Pharaoh with half-indifferent curiosity.

"Perhaps not, great god," answered one of the huntsmen. "He is greatly torn, but he is a young man and very strong."

"I will make him a free man and a captain if he lives," said Pharaoh, "for this is my first lion, and it is fitting that the slave should remember this day. I hit him square behind the shoulder and was not afraid, fierce though he was. I will have pictures made of this hunt, and on other days I will kill more lions. Men must fetch them from the Libyan desert if there are none to be found in the hills. They say that a lion has not been seen here for thirty years."

This being what the company was thinking, a dead silence followed Pharaoh's last remark, and those who supposed themselves unnoticed glanced at Ai. His lean countenance remained perfectly unmoved, but he stepped forward a pace and bowed to Pharaoh with a flourish. "I thank the good god," said he, "because in rewarding the slave he approves my service. As it was I who placed this young man in Pharaoh's chariot, it is through my care that the king is safe and has slain the lion."

"Am I indeed to owe you the lion?" asked Pharaoh maliciously. "There is no end to your care, my lord, it seems."

A half-smile crossed the faces of those who dared to express their feelings, but Ai merely bowed again to the king and said, "Honor paid to this slave is paid to me, and with your permission, I will let men know that such is the fact." Two men immediately stepped forward to lay their cloaks on Hor, while the slave with the water passed his hand under the wounded man's head and put to his lips the silver cup which he carried for the exclusive use of Pharaoh himself. Ai saw it and smiled. "Honor is indeed paid to me," he said.

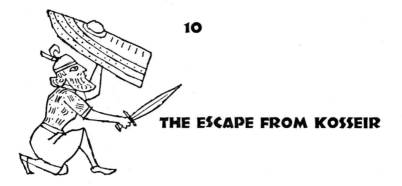

10

THE ESCAPE FROM KOSSEIR

IT was the siesta time when Maru came down to the docks and found the Nubian porters lounging in the shade while they refreshed themselves with flat, dry cakes of bread and muddy water. They watched him lazily as he strolled past the boats by the landing, casting over them an anxious glance which he vainly endeavored to conceal. "Look at the little scribe," called one of them to another jeeringly. "How neat he looks in his pretty white kilt and with his pen behind his ear!"

"See him blush!" remarked a second, spitting out a stone he had found in his bread and stretching out a long arm for the water. "That's right, my dear! Take out the sweet pen now and throw it away! Did they beat your poor little back until you ran off to go for a soldier? What a shame!"

This being rather near the truth, Maru blushed more hotly than ever and walked away, fairly breaking into a run as one group of Nubians after another began to laugh.

"Now then, boy! Look where you are going," cried a solid citizen, catching him by the arm as he raced toward an alley. "Can't a man come peacefully down to his boat without being knocked right off the wharf?"

"You have a boat?" stammered Maru. "Do you — do you need a boy?"

"Of course not," said the solid man contemptuously. "Go home to Mother." He turned Maru's face toward the alley and gave a strong push which sent him flying. Maru could hear the Nubians roar as he disappeared from view.

"So you want to run away, do you, my boy?" asked a hoarse voice as Maru was using the edge of the offending white kilt to wipe the blood off his scraped knees. Maru looked up and arose slowly, uncertain how to answer and not much liking what he saw.

The man standing over him was a very dark-colored Egyptian with a dash of Nubian blood visible in his thick lips and the heavy contour of his face. His legs were short and a little bowed, but a formidable chest and arms gave him a misshapen appearance, rather like one of those apes Pharaoh collected in tribute from time to time. He grinned, showing discolored teeth, and inquired once more in beery tones, "Want to see life and grow rich, is that it? How would you like to go with a caravan to Kosseir?"

"Er — I think I must go home now." Maru flattened himself against the wall of the alley and tried to sidle past him. The man put out a great, rough hand, and gripped his arm.

"Oh no you don't! I thought you wanted to have adventures and see the world."

Maru squirmed and writhed, but without the slightest effect, until in desperation he bent down his head and bit at the back of the detaining hand.

This produced a stunning box on the ear, followed by another and another. "You would, would you?" said the beery voice as things swam before him. "Take that to teach you a lesson, and come along with me." Maru felt himself dragged forward, seeing through a mist of tears the guffawing Nubians. He was pushed up a gangplank, felt a horny foot in his posterior, shot forward, hit his head against something hard, and for the moment knew no more.

He was awakened by the sound of someone groaning from a dream in which one of the servants was giving him his daily bath. After a minute, he opened his eyes and the groaning stopped. A douche of water caught him full in the face before his eyes had time to focus, causing him to gasp and retch feebly, putting up a hand to cover his face.

"I don't much like it," somebody was grumbling. "If I had my way we would drop him over the side and no questions asked. What possessed you to pick up a boy like that from the public dock?"

"There he was just when I needed a boy," protested another. "Do you think I can afford to buy me a slave every time one happens to drop dead? Pass me the water."

Maru opened his eyes and stared wildly at what came within his range of vision. He was lying somewhere in the back part of a boat, looking up at the legs of an Ethiopian, who stood on a small high platform handling the steering oar. Maru made a little movement to sit up, but desisted with a moan as he felt a sudden twinge of pain in his head.

"What's your name, boy?" It was the dark man bending over him.

"Maru."

"You have got a new master, Maru," said the dark man threateningly, "and in case you do not like it, here is my stick." He produced a stick and made whistling noises through the air. "Now are you going to lie here quiet and cause no trouble?"

"Yes." Maru shut his aching eyes.

"Leave the boy alone, Satmi," grumbled the other voice from behind him. "From the looks of him, you might just as well have thrown him to the crocodiles."

"He'll be all right at Coptos," said Satmi carelessly. "You had better get some sleep, boy. Tomorrow there will be work."

Maru drifted off into half-unconsciousness as the big boat swung down the river, vaguely aware of the bales of cargo on which he was lying and the pale stars in the evening sky above. Now and then a lookout man in the bows would warn of a sandbank, and the voice of the Ethiopian would arise in a half-chanted answer as he leaned upon the creaking oar. On these occasions Maru was roused from his vague slumber to notice that the moon was up, was high, or was waning as the night wore on. Before dawn he awoke completely, shivering and hungry, and sat up in the gray light to take stock of his surroundings.

He was lying on a heap of old mats thrown down on top of some cargo so carefully swathed that its outlines were hardly visible. All around him lay jars of various shapes, piled in heaps on their sides and packed between bundles so closely that except on the rowers' benches and the little cat-walk between them there was no clear space to be seen. A familiar creak from astern caused him to glance upward and catch sight of a patched brown sail gliding slowly past the edge of the boat. He jumped to his feet, picked his way carefully across the cargo, and knelt on a rowing bench to look out over the water. Not twenty yards off, another cargo boat was going upstream with the help of the wind. Maru actually opened his mouth to give a shout, but shut it again determinedly. Tears gathered in his eyes, however, as

he watched the distance between the two boats increasing
until the other disappeared around a big bend in the stream.

"That's right," said an approving voice behind him. "If
you had called out, they would have killed you. The captain is frightened that there may be trouble over you in
Thebes."

A Nubian boy of about Maru's own age was sitting behind him on the catwalk with his knees up to his chin, engaged in biting pieces off a lump of dark bread that looked as
hard as any brick. He grinned as Maru gulped, put his
bread down before him on the deck, and hammered off a
sizable portion. "Here," he said abruptly, thrusting it at
Maru. "Have something to eat."

Maru took it without a word because his voice was not yet
under control. He worried at it, succeeded in biting off a
piece, and began to chew. It was not good, but it was quite
sustaining. After he had ground up a few mouthfuls and
swallowed them, he felt distinctly better.

"Who are you?" he inquired, reflecting that he had never
seen a more dusty, or more knobbly little figure in his life.

The Nubian, whose mouth was stopped with bread, took
a large, unchewed piece out in order to say concisely,

"Donkey Boy," before he popped it back in and began to work on it.

"What's your name, then?" persisted Maru.

"That's what they call me, because I drive the donkeys. It's not a bad life, and plenty of masters are worse than Satmi is."

"Shall I drive donkeys too?"

"That's what I came to talk to you about," replied Donkey Boy, nodding his shock head solemnly at Maru. "A man like me has to look after his own interests, seeing that Satmi has worse than no sense at all when he has drunk a little beer. Think of picking you up like that on the wharf with all the porters watching! Why don't you go over the side before we all get into trouble about you? There's a landing on that shore." He pointed at a rickety little dock, near which a huddle of huts and a clump of untidy looking palms marked some sort of settlement. "Well, what about it?"

Maru shook his head. "I can't go home," he said. "My uncle — "

"Don't tell me!" interrupted Donkey Boy hastily. "I don't want to know who he is. A man like me has to keep himself out of trouble."

"Don't worry," said Maru. "I think they may not come after me because there would be complications when I was found."

Donkey Boy heaved a sigh of obvious relief. "It's not bad with the convoys," he said, pursing his lips judicially, "and when Satmi gets away from the beer shops, he's a good-tempered man. Can you use any weapons?"

"Why, yes," said Maru, surprised at the question. "We were trained every day with the bow and arrow or the spear."

"You'll do," said Donkey Boy grinning. "Ever handled a donkey?"

"I've driven a horse."

"You just wait," said Donkey Boy. "You just wait and see!"

People were stirring in the cabin amidships and on the small forward platform. Maru learned that there were a couple of traders on board in addition to Satmi, besides the captain and the Ethiopians who made up the crew. There was nothing to do but to sit and warm in the sun, lazily watching the river and the various activities upon it. Women were already at their washing, and the clop of their regular beating could be heard around every little bend in the stream. Fishermen were out in tarred reed boats, or sometimes in larger ones in which half a dozen men would be splitting their fish and hanging them on the yards to dry in the sun. Market boats of all sizes filled with big grass baskets of produce were rowed by chattering men or women out of the mouths of irrigation canals. Traders passed up and down, loaded to the very roof of their cabins. The abusive shouts of boatmen rose in the air, mingled with the lowing of cattle, and the chanting of oarsmen. On the bank in rough temporary stocks a big wooden boat was being constructed. Farther down came another, and another. The brown or whitewashed walls of houses began to appear instead of fields. Far off in the distance a white wall flanked by brightly colored towers came into view.

"The city of Coptos," said Donkey Boy, pointing, "and there is the temple of Min."

The wharves of Coptos stretched literally for miles along the river, the outer ones crowded with humbler, local vessels, and the inner ones bustling with porters, donkeys, overseers,

scribes, and a complicated assortment of wares. The air was
thick with the scent of frankincense and spices from Arabia.

 Little crates of bright birds,
monkeys, and even young
giraffes came up from Kosseir on the Red Sea, together
with ivory, gold, and a special collection of carefully
protected trees. Maru had
seen such sights before when
Pharaoh received his tribute,
but the jumble, the noise,
and the confusion was utterly new. He was staring, fasci-
nated at everything, when a stick poked him sharply in the
ribs. Satmi was standing behind him.

"Come on, boy," he said, gesturing toward the wharf-
side. "Work."

The next days passed in a hustle and bustle of loading, un-
loading, and getting familiar with donkeys. Maru discovered precisely what Donkey Boy had meant when he had
nodded his head and said, "You just wait and see!" Donkeys,
he found, did not kick often, but they bit. Sometimes his
would be as good as gold, standing patiently to be loaded.
Suddenly they reached round and nipped for no reason, or
gave a shake when the girths were being tightened, so that
the paniers shifted and everything had to be replaced. They
would suffer themselves to be piled with an incredible load
of jars of ointment, cheap beads, bronze spearheads, and
other treasures dear to the Africans of Punt. After carrying
these for an hour or so, with no sign of weakness, they
would suddenly refuse to move, presenting no uncovered
surface to their furious drover except a rump impervious to

blows and insensitive even to frantic prodding with a spear. Over and over again Donkey Boy had to come to the rescue with a strange cry which seemed to soothe donkeys, and with an expert hand in their ears.

"You'll learn," he always repeated. "Don't get so excited." But whether because of a natural antipathy to donkeys, or because so much else was strange and new, Maru did not immediately learn.

The convoy consisted of six groups of about a dozen donkeys, each with its owner, who might act as drover or, like Satmi, as a guard. Each group provided one soldier, and there were extra weapons packed on the donkey's backs. Satmi gave Maru a bow when he saw that he could use it, and he seemed to consider that the boy's skill with this weapon had won him a right to be left alone. As Donkey Boy had said, Satmi was good-humored enough in places where he could obtain no beer.

From Coptos to Kosseir on the Red Sea was a five-day journey through a cleft in the barren hills over waterless rocks and blistering sand. The men rose before dawn and marched to some spot where a little shade for man and beast was known to be obtainable. Here they unloaded, watered the donkeys, and spent the hot hours of the day in trying to sleep or in fighting with flies, which appeared in the midst of the lifeless desert as though some devil were in them. When the sun sank low, the donkeys were loaded again with much slipping and cursing, and a second march through the gathering dark was begun. Maru found this the worst part of the day, as the burning earth gave back its heat until the air was like an oven. Even in sandals, his feet grew sore from the hot sand.

On the third night out, there was a pleasant diversion in

camping by a well which seemed cool and gave out a grati-
fying splash when a bucket was hastily lowered into it. For
the first time since setting out, Maru could drink his fill.
When he had watered the donkeys, he was even able to re-
move his sandals and soak his sore and dusty feet, which he
found more perfectly refreshing than anything he had ever
known.

Satmi evidently felt the same way because he grinned
across in friendly fashion. "Well, youngster," said he, "how
do you enjoy seeing life?"

"Very much," said Maru enthusiastically, reveling in the
glorious wetness of his feet and his temporary freedom from
donkeys.

"Bear no grudge?"

"Not a bit since you put away your stick."

There was a short companionable silence. Maru put his
hands into the water and began to splash it up his arms.

"I was thinking of shipping you off as a slave to Arabia,"
said Satmi unexpectedly. "Don't want to get into trouble
for kidnaping you."

"You won't get into trouble through me," Maru assured
him.

Satmi grunted. "All right," he said, "as long as you know
you can go back home when you like."

"As soon as you get near the next beer house, I shall be
off," said Maru with meaning.

Satmi gave a hoarse rumble of a laugh. "You learn fast,
boy," he said. "Surely by then you will know how to hide
from the stick."

He got up and hitched his shield into position. "My
watch, I think," called he to the convoy captain. Maru
yawned. Now that his feet were cool, he felt desperately

sleepy. Donkey Boy, who never seemed to be too hot, had curled up half an hour before. In a few hours it would be time to move again. He had a moment's delicious consciousness of relaxing fully before he was asleep.

Maru dreamed that he had lost his donkeys. One moment they were standing still, apparently hobbled. In the next, with the malice of their kind, they had wriggled themselves free and departed, leaving nothing but a derisive bray to remember them by. Maru woke up suddenly and was conscious of a violent indignation against donkeys, even as it flashed across his mind that what he had heard was actually a stifled scream. With a loud shout, he leaped to his feet, seized his bow, and loosed an arrow point-blank at a figure that had straightened up and was lifting its arm as he arose. In a moment startled cries were mingled with fierce yells, and the braying of donkeys made inextricable confusion through the camp.

There were but thirteen men with the caravan, but even the drovers slept with their weapons beside them and knew how to use them well. No one but Maru was new on this sort of convoy, so that all had the sense to leave the donkeys to shift for themselves while they assembled to fight for their lives. The desert marauders who had attacked them were armed with long knives, more convenient for midnight assassination than a stand-up fight. Man for man they were no match for the people of the convoy, once the camp had been fully aroused. One huge fellow came yelling through the dark at Maru, who clean missed him in his excitement, since his hand was shaking from the reaction of having actually killed a man. Before he could fit a second arrow to the string, his enemy was upon him. In desperation Maru slashed with his bow across the big man's face, driving him back a little. At that very instant Donkey Boy's javelin flashed past and buried itself deep in the enemy's chest.

"Get back here," shouted Donkey Boy, seizing another weapon. Maru ran for cover behind a little barricade of merchandise.

The short, sharp struggle was almost over. The desert robbers had slashed loose a few donkeys, grabbed a few bales, and departed, leaving several of their number groaning upon the ground. By the light of torches, people were soon rounding up their animals, dressing flesh wounds, and taking a rough count of the damage to their wares.

"Where is Satmi?" called the captain of the convoy suddenly. "Was he not sentry?" Maru shuddered violently, remembering that first scream.

Satmi was quite dead from a knife thrust through his back. They dug a hole for him and laid him in it, while Maru wandered away with Donkey Boy, sobered and sickened, feeling young and very much alone.

There was no sleep possible for the rest of that night. Presently the water skins were being filled, and the signal was given for the donkeys to be loaded. Maru saw a barrel-chested man with a knife scar across one cheek approaching, while two or three others lounged along behind. With a beating heart, he felt cautiously beside him for his bow.

"You slaves there," cried the big man roughly, "get along and fall in behind my drover. You belong to me now, and I stand no nonsense. Hurry up!" He made a great slash in the direction of Donkey Boy, who stood nearest, and caught him full across the stern as he dived for safety underneath his animals. Two of the onlookers broke into a laugh.

"Stop!" cried Maru loudly, snatching up his bow and leveling it, hoping that his trembling would not betray how nervous he really felt. "I am no slave, and Satmi never called me such. The boy and the donkeys both are mine now he is dead."

"Why you little monkey!" said the big man violently. "Do you think you are the only one in camp who knows how to shoot?"

"If anybody picks up his bow, I shall put an arrow through your chest," retorted Maru. "Donkey Boy, look out and see if anyone is threatening from behind!"

"Leave the boys alone," called out the convoy captain, hurrying over with a few supporters at his side. "We all owe our lives to the little Egyptian; and if he wants to say he is free, why, let him do so. Keep your arrows for the desert marauders. We may yet need every fighter we have got."

The big fellow hesitated, but Maru's bow was still ready. "You'll not get away with it," he said scowling, "when we come to Kosseir. I'll teach you who's free there and who is not." He walked off to vent his ill temper on his own unfortunate drover, who was soon heard yelling amid the sound of blows.

Maru finished the loading and then took his bow in his hand as he walked beside the donkeys, keeping a very respectable distance behind his new enemy. The heat was telling on the animals that day, and everybody felt the lack of sleep. Nevertheless, when they encamped for the night, Maru and Donkey Boy took turns watching and both were sure that their wakefulness had been observed. By morning both boys were thoroughly weary, and were frightened of what might be done to them in the port that lay ahead. Maru, who had been thinking over things carefully, dropped back in the morning's march to talk to the convoy captain, walking at the point of danger in the rear of the line.

"What did Satmi say about me in the convoy?" he asked.

The captain shrugged his shoulders. "That you were a rich man's son who had run away from Thebes, and that he was half of a mind to dispose of you, lest you get him into trouble," he said.

"If I were disposed of now," answered Maru meaningly, "someone would certainly talk, and that might be very bad."

The captain looked at him keenly. "So I thought," he admitted. "In any case, we owe you something for saving our lives."

"Look," said Maru, "will you make a bargain? Give me the Nubian boy and the load of one ass, and take the rest of Satmi's goods for yourself. All I ask is a little protection in the port of Kosseir."

"See here," said the captain protesting, "Kosseir is not a nursery. It's no place at all for a boy on his own, and there's nowhere it leads to. There is no other place on all this sea which is not utterly savage. You may sail out with a trader, but when he has finished his business, there is no port you can come back to except Kosseir. Even that will seem better than being enslaved by some black chieftain who decorates his beehive hut with skulls. There is no way out of Kosseir, and once you have enemies there, you are done for. Personally, I could not afford to make any, not if Satmi's donkeys were loaded with pure gold."

There was a frightened silence while Maru thought things over. Presently he plucked up his courage and said in slightly trembling tones, "Can't you even give me a little advice?"

The captain looked at him more kindly. "We are going straight down to the docks with this convoy, and you should be safe on the quays there until it is dark. If in that time you can get passage to Punt or Arabia, take it. You can always hope that no one will be waiting for you back in Kosseir. I will take over Satmi's donkeys and pay you an honest value if you ever get back to the beer shop in Coptos which is marked with the sign of the red goose."

He spoke encouragingly, yet Maru knew from a certain pity in his tone that the captain thought little of his chances. He swallowed several times before he could answer, but brought out finally, "I expect I shall not need Satmi's goods, but I shall inquire for you at the Red Goose all the same." He hastened his step to get away from the captain before betraying the extent of his helplessness and fear.

They reached Kosseir in the forenoon and found it an incredibly tough little settlement made up of shanties huddled around squares that seemed to be regarded as communal garbage dumps. Brown men, black men, and bearded men of all shades lounged in the alleys, all wearing knives and looking like wicked tomcats with torn ears. The only two women Maru saw were screaming and tearing each other's hair in the roadway, while an interested crowd was looking on and making bets. In one doorway a man lay dead with a knife through him, while people stepped over him as

though they did not notice what was there. Everything shimmered in a stinking, close, unendurable heat in which the pungent odors of Arabian spices were mingled with garbage, rotting fish, and drying seaweed, together with all the various smells of unwashed humanity.

It was a relief to come out on to the docks, filthy and crowded as they were. There was something tremendous in looking out of that tiny, stinking port at the clean sparkling stretches of the sea. Maru had an instantaneous impression of infinite width and glorious blue which was beyond anything he had ever dreamed. He drew in his breath and stared.

"Maru!" Donkey Boy brought him abruptly down to earth by nudging him. "The ships for Punt have gone without us. Look there!"

Sure enough, five ships were standing out, their pinkish-brown sails gradually filling as they caught the breeze that was cut off from Kosseir by the bay. They seemed almost, if not quite, in earshot, but they were definitely gone. Maru watched them turning slowly southward toward the pathway of the midday sun. His heart sank utterly, but he forced himself to say in careful tones, "Very well. We shall have to go to Arabia instead."

Beneath his usual dusty brown, Donkey Boy was a sickish, greenish color. "We can't," he whispered. "The Arabian ships aren't leaving for five days." His eyes actually filled with tears.

It was the sight of tears which spurred Maru to action. He looked desperately around. "Come on! There is at least something going on down there."

The ship to which he was pointing was a large and clumsy freighter, more sturdily built than the Nile boats, fully

decked, and with her bulwarks raised. Some altercation was
going on between a man seated on the yard-arm and one
halfway down the gangplank with a bundle on his back.
"Three years!" the latter was yelling, "Three years with
that son of ill omen! Why, I wouldn't sail to Arabia with
him, let alone to the mouth of the Nile!" He shook his fist
at the man on the yard-arm and disappeared amid a crowd of
onlookers. Donkey Boy watched him in puzzled fascination, the tears still standing wet on his cheeks.

"Three years!" said he. "Three years to the mouth of
the Nile! What can he mean?"

"But I know!" exclaimed Maru suddenly. "Why, of
course! I had forgotten, but I always knew about that ship.
They are going southward, hugging the shore on their right
hand. When they have sailed a season, they are to land,
plant corn, and reap it, repairing their boat meanwhile, and
replenishing their other stores. Then they will set off again
and sail on for another season until the land turns north-
ward. After three years or four they hope to go round
Africa and reach the mouth of the Nile."

"I don't believe it," said Donkey Boy flatly, shaking his
head with conviction. "They will simply be eaten by monsters or sail over the edge of the world." He looked gloomily at the big boat, in which men were unlashing the sail and
setting up the steering oar.

"It is the way out of Kosseir," insisted Maru. "I do believe there is a good chance that Africa will turn out to be
round. In my uncle's palace — "

"Your uncle's palace!" said Donkey Boy feebly, putting
up a half-protesting hand. "A man like me — "

"Has to keep out of trouble," finished Maru rapidly.
"Donkey Boy, if you and I are to go into undiscovered seas

as comrades, I would like you to know who I really am. Now and then there are conspiracies in Pharaoh's palace, as is natural enough when the king has many wives and many sons. It has happened before and may happen again that a prince, though innocent, may learn too much of such dark dealings to be safe. So it was with me. When we sail up the Nile together, you and I will be grown and altered and may be known by different names. I think I shall call myself Sinuhe in memory of a prince who fled in earlier times. Come on, or they will be taking up the gangplank and leave us like trapped rats in stinking Kosseir."

He tucked his arm in Donkey Boy's and tugged at him gently. The little Nubian looked this way and that at the docks and the alleys, but he yielded to the insistent pressure and followed along. Arm in arm they passed up the gangplank and jumped over the bulwarks. There were shouts back and forth to the yardarm, but the two boys did not reappear. Instead, a couple of sailors pulled in the gangplank. The oars splashed in the water, and the ship set out for the Nile around Africa.

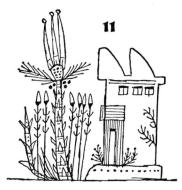

11

THE TREE

HE NEVER KNEW who his father had been, and he could
not perfectly remember his mother. He slept in no special
corner of his own, but just where he could, most frequently
in the workshop where the gardening tools were repaired.
Now and then he was issued a loincloth, and he usually had
enough left of the old one to tie a strip around his head
against the sun. He was the least of all the slaves in Pharaoh's
garden, and he did not even have a name. The women and
children laughed at his queer shape and called him Monkey.
Overseers said, "You, there!" or laid on with a stick. The
other gardeners simply ignored him, or kicked him aside like
a dog when he got in their way.

During a great part of the year he worked at buckets,
lifting water until his hands, calloused as they were, would
mark the rope with blood. His whole back was seamed
with welts from many beatings; and it might have appeared
a marvel, if any man had cared to wonder at it, that he could
endure so much and live so long. If he had been set to work
in the more beautiful parts of the garden, he would have
been driven harder and might have died, as others did, in a
year or two. Fortunately even the overseers were ashamed

of him and used to place him near the stinking rubbish pits
outside the wall of the garden, or in other hidden places,
where for hours together they did not need to come. This
had saved him, while in time a special pride of his own had
grown within him. Alone of all the slaves of Pharaoh, he
owned a tree.

Egypt was a poor land for trees. The floods destroyed
them, and the hot, dry time when the earth cracked open
withered them away. So precious were they that no man
might cut one, even on his own land, without asking permission to do so. The best trees were all imported and grew in
rich men's gardens. Pharaoh's came by ship from Lebanon,
or up the Red Sea from distant Punt and over the desert,
with a train of water carriers to moisten their roots. A

collar of solid gold would not have bought one, yet this meanest of the slaves in the garden nursed one he had some right to call his own.

It happened, while this slave was still a lad and had not yet been put to the heaviest labor, that the glorious mind of Pharaoh had conceived of a lake especially created for the pleasure of his wife. A boat of the finest cedarwood inlaid with gold should ride on it, in which twenty girls were to row and sing in chorus to delight the queen. A gay painted summerhouse on the shore must look over the water at masses of green beneath the cliffs of the western des-ert, mysteriously purple in the shades of the setting sun. These beautiful thoughts Pharaoh proclaimed from his gold throne in his hall of audience, wearing the blue crown and holding the glittering symbols of his divinity. These commands the chief minister heard, groveling on the floor before his king and god as was proper. These he proclaimed in his turn to the Master of Pharaoh's Boats, the Steward of Pharaoh's Summerhouses, the Director of Pharaoh's Pleasures, and all such people as were thought worthy to hear the good news from his exalted lips. Next, these gave audience to lesser persons, and they to others. In a little time extra slaves were set to make mattocks or baskets for the carrying of earth, while droves of wretched laborers were being herded into boats in the Delta to join with those stationed at Thebes on the glorious work.

That was a bad time, and the slave always remembered it

with a shudder. Indeed, his twisted shape was mainly due to carrying those heavy loads before he was grown. Many died, for besides the labor, there was sickness that spread like wildfire through the wretched temporary barracks, where at night the men had scarcely room to stretch full length upon the floor. Soon there was a gravedigger gang, for such people were not worth the trouble of embalming. Crowds of new slaves came in every month and died like flies, while a few became seasoned, only to collapse at last under the incessant toil. First a vast basin had to be hollowed, and the earth carried out in baskets to spread on the banks or farther away. There were great boulders in this soil, some of which fifty men could hardly drag up the bank and off into the desert. Besides the lake, a canal must be constructed to bring water and to let it flow out again across the land. An island was made in the middle, and on the western bank a series of hummocks, so that the trees might rise toward the cliffs as Pharaoh's beautiful thoughts had imagined them. Long before the banks were ready, trees arrived and were laid by the hundreds in temporary trenches, while the head gardeners inspected their watering and cursed the delay.

It was over at last, the mud barracks knocked down, and the rubbish and filth of the slave camp tidied away. Quick-growing bushes had been planted by thousands to clothe the slopes with green while the trees were young. Forget-me-nots, celandine, and other wild flowers had been set out in masses by the water. By next year all traces of man's miseries would be smothered in a fairyland of blossom.

Gangs of slaves who were no longer needed had been sent to the quarries, a dreadful fate which this one only escaped because he was considered too ill. When he did not die after all, they sent him staggering down to the lake where men were planting in groups of five, two digging holes, two carrying water, and one doing the skilled work. The trees were by now in poor condition, and it was considered better to discard a doubtful one than to be blamed for planting those which did not grow. As a matter of course, the importers had supplied twice as many as would be required. Dead ones were thrown on a heap, whence they disappeared with the connivance of the overseers, who understood that the men must do some sort of cooking now and again. It was with this idea in mind that the slave, tugging one night at the brush pile, found himself with a tree in his hands which he felt sure could yet live.

His first thought was to throw it back and find another. His second was to plunge his nose deep among its branches and enjoy the smell. It was a cypress, which he had never before seen closely, since he and his gang had been planting peach trees in clumps along the shore. It came into his mind that if he could plant it, he might take pleasure in passing it from time to time. Outside the high wall of the palace garden was a small space, half concealed by the belt of flowering shrubs that screened the rubbish pits. It was on the far side of the path and very private. Yet, he thought, I can find excuses for coming by here. He went down quietly to the lakeside and fetched a bucket so that he could plant exactly as he had seen the gardeners do.

Later on, when he was set to watering the garden, he only remembered the little tree now and again. After a few months, he forgot it completely until the next growing season came to remind him. The tree was still there and had

bright little tips to its branches, which were more beautifully
scented than ever before. For the very first time he felt a
sense of possession and liked it. Nobody will beat me, he
thought, if I root you up and throw you away. Reflecting
thus that its tender growth was by his permission, he began
to feel an anxious pride, as a man does in his child. He
formed the habit of looking at it daily and giving it water,
while he calculated its growth in a twelvemonth, or wondered how tall it would be in several years.

It was not until seven growing seasons had passed by that
an incident taught him that his tree was no longer a child,
but had become a god. That year there was sickness among
the slaves of the palace, as was often the case in the outbuildings where lower servants lived seven or eight to a
room. One day when the slave came to ask for his daily
rations, he found not the hag who usually cooked for him,
but a youngish, shabby girl.

It was the custom of the stewards in Pharaoh's household
to give the slaves their supplies at about the time of the full
moon. Each had his measure of oil, his portion of onions or
salt fish, and his small sack of grain. This went to the wives,
who ground and baked and doled out with careful planning
so that the ration might last until the moon was full again.
If a slave had no woman, he gave up his food to the wife of
another, who paid herself as a matter of course by pilfering
from his stock. The wretched hag who fed this slave not
only starved him, but daily made him the target of her
shrill abuse. It had become a penance to fetch his bread,
which was doled out in ever smaller portions as his dumb
endurance made the woman bold.

The slave slouched up to the doorway and extended his
hand, while the girl with a sullen scowl on her pinched face

put into it his miserable allotment. She was expecting to shrink away and scream an answer when he bullied her, but to her surprise, he took it with a heavy sigh and turned away. Starvation was preferable to public jeers, he knew.

He was halfway across the yard when the girl came running after him. "Here!" she said abruptly, and slipped into his hand another piece of bread.

He twisted it between his fingers slowly as he thought things out. "You will be beaten," he mumbled after a moment, staring at it as if it were some strange delicacy from Pharaoh's kitchen.

The girl shrugged in her sulky fashion. "Not today," said she, half ashamed of her impulse and angry at being seen in public with this twisted mockery of a man. "The woman is far too sick to care." With that she turned around and ran away.

She had shown him kindness, and she had bothered to answer when he spoke, and besides all this, there was the bread. He puzzled over his feelings while he chewed it slowly, exploring each mouthful with caution for lumps too hard for his teeth. By midday, he had come to the conclusion that he would offer her something, though this was easier said than done, since he had not even a small clay amulet of his own. After a great deal more thinking, he went very reluctantly and broke a beautiful, scented branch off his tree.

Nothing was private in the slave quarters. Since morning the girl had already endured a good deal in the way of remarks about her handsome new lover. If he had brought her a posy from the marshes, she might have thrown it out indignantly and sent him about his business without delay. Unfortunately, the branch was far too queer a present, and

she took it, screeching with laughter, from door to door. By
nightfall, it was common knowledge that he had broken a
piece off one of Pharaoh's valuable trees.

The story did not reach the overseer until morning, but
when it did, he took his stick and went to investigate. Now
and then flowers were picked before they were quite faded.
It was even possible when fruit was gathered to look occasionally another way. Trees, however, were Pharaoh's
pride and must never be damaged. Besides, the slave should
not have been near them in the course of his work.

The inquiry started with a beating that very soon in-
duced the slave to confess his sins. "It was only a tree by
the rubbish pits," cried he.

"There is no tree by the rubbish pits," retorted the overseer, and laid on harder.

"Suppose we make him show us," one of the men who
held the slave suggested good-naturedly. "He is really too

stupid to explain clearly where he has been."

They let him get up and lead the way miserably to the little space beneath the bushes and the wall.

"Why, there is a tree here after all!" exclaimed the overseer. "This is quite extraordinary. I must ask the head gardener where he would like it, as there is no use leaving it in a place like this." He went away with his men after pointing out to the slave his daily allotment of work.

All day long the slave struggled sullenly with the buckets, aching in every limb and brooding wretchedly. By now the tree had become more than a possession; it was something that made him a man, not a beast, in his secret heart. When evening came, he gathered a handful of berries he had heard his fellow slaves say were poisonous. Some overseers who pressed their men too hard had died mysteriously, but the slave was far too humble for any such ideas. His thought was to lie out under the tree that night and kill himself.

It was peaceful close to the wall, protected by the bushes and hearing the scented branches of his tree rustling above his head. He felt comforted by the whispering sound and did not eat the berries. "I will not actually be moved," the tree seemed to say. "You had better wait."

By a miracle, the very next morning there was another overseer, a fierce new broom with an even larger stick. "Because the old one has the sickness," shouted he, "is not a reason for you to slacken in your work."

There were more blows that week than usual, but the slave did not mind them. When he heard the old one was actually dead, he felt a fierce joy mixed with awe. "There is a powerful god in my tree," he muttered. "How strange that I had not known it until it killed this man!"

Time passed quietly thenceforth, until the tree had grown

so tall that the slave was constantly frightened lest the gardeners notice it. Fortunately the queen perceived it first from her boat of cedarwood, in which the girls were singing softly as they rowed about. "As I look around this paradise," said she to Pharaoh, "it is that single cypress by the distant white wall which pleases me most greatly. How perfectly you have placed it at the end of the gap the canal makes between the trees!"

A man who is also a god does not expect in one short lifetime to think all of his wondrous thoughts himself, but has to delegate to his servants many of the treasures of his mind. Thus Pharaoh was pleased to accept this part of his own plan, and he readily answered, "I am particularly happy that it gives you pleasure because it is in such details that I best express the exquisite perfection of my taste. I will send a gold ring to the chief among my gardeners for his care in fulfilling my desires."

After this the tree grew freely, and no one hindered it. If the slave was seen watering it from time to time, it was considered a part of his duty and occasioned no remark. The little space between the tree and the wall was now his lair, and in it, he had even accumulated a few possessions. He had found a ragged old cloak for cold nights, had laid a soft bed of rushes, and had brought in pretty pebbles or flowers to please his tree.

Like all gods, the tree was quite capricious. A certain charm might be good for many days if repeated to it exactly; yet eventually it wore out after some fashion, and the slave would get into trouble until he had changed his spell. He took to asking people about spells and became quite learned in them, so that now and then he was called upon for magic when people were ill. This brought him presents which he faithfully buried by the tree, keeping back nothing. Better still, it earned him gratitude. Old slaves were not very common among the lower servants, and his fellows began to feel curiously proud of him for living on. Even the overseers became friendly in time and seldom did more than whistle their sticks through the air. "This work is too much for you," said the latest one quite kindly as he found him struggling with the bucket. "We must give you something light, in the kitchen perhaps, where there will be scraps better suited to your toothless gums."

"I like — this work," protested the old man gasping, but the overseer only laughed a little as he moved away.

He took his trouble to the tree that night as usual, but for the first time for many years it did not comfort him. "You are too young," he muttered into its branches, "and do not know what it feels like when your strength begins to fail." The tree answered nothing, for there was not the slightest breeze and no combination of spells would seem to produce one. At last when dawn came, the slave saw that his god despised him in its youthful strength and had cast him off completely. He scattered his rushes into the pit, folded his cloak, buried the bright stones under a covering of earth, and went away.

He was not the slightest use in the kitchen, where the chattering dazed him and the stuffy heat of the fires gave him headaches all day long. People were always pushing him aside to get at things behind him. The head chef openly pitied himself for being saddled with a man who was queer in the head. They let him try to sweep the floor, but then said he was too old to carry the rubbish and sent a boy to take it out to the pits. At night they kindly gave him a very warm corner near the embers of the hateful fire, where he lay feeling stifled and sickened by the heavy smell of fats.

After a while their patience wore thin with him, and they found him a nuisance. "Stop poking around!" yelled the head chef crossly one day as he was trying to sweep.

The old man tottered to a corner and sat down with his hands to his bursting temples, groaning to himself.

"Phew!" said the head baker, taking up one of the little fans which were used to keep the fire glowing and trying to cool off his face. "I really never felt heat like this before."

"It's just as bad outside," said a boy staggering in with water. "The sky is a gray-blue color, and there is a queer ring round the sun."

"It is the end of the world!" cried a young barbarian sharply.

"Nonsense!" retorted the head chef, feeling that it was his duty to set a tone for the kitchen. "Once in my father's time there was a flood in heaven, so that water poured out of it for hours, turned his house to mud, and washed it away. Frogs descended, he said, with the water, but in a few days they died and stank. This was a marvel that started with a queer ring round the sun."

A slave looked up from a duck that he was turning on a spit above the flame. "That is only rain," he said with scorn. "In Troy, we have it often." He never let the kitchen forget that his father was king of a few miserable huts somewhere by the ocean to the north.

"I suppose it rains crocodiles in Troy!" said someone scornfully. It was long ago established in the kitchen that every story about Troy was to be taken as untrue.

One of the baker's boys, who was bringing over a fresh batch of cakes for frying, chose this moment to faint dead away and fell with a clatter, dropping the dough from his tray and collapsing on top of it.

The head baker burst into a wail. "It wants but half an hour to Pharaoh's dinner!" cried he in dismay. "Bring me some more quickly! Old fool in the corner, come here and clean up this mess!" He bustled about, sweat streaming from his forehead, and harried his underlings.

In the confusion of getting Pharaoh's dinner, the kitchen was a turmoil. Carvers clamored for the meat, decorators snatched at the breadstuffs, beautifully dressed waiters rushed in and out, swearing horribly at the kitchen servants. Everyone was slipping and sweating in the terrible heat. When the meal was over, the slaves all straggled into the courtyard without touching the scraps that were their usual food. Even the water boy, who was famous for his appetite, declared himself revolted by the very idea of eating anything. They were content to fan themselves, dip head or hands in water, and stare exhausted at the leaden sky.

The old man, his throbbing head clutched in his hands, tottered off around the corner. For the first time since he had come to the kitchen, nobody bothered to ask where in the world he thought he was going. He went along the familiar path by the gardeners' quarters, where a few wretched women and children stared listlessly after him, and passed out of the small side gate leading to the pits.

The tree was taller than ever and looked as though its young pride felt no concern with stunted, elderly things. He did not even venture to address a spell to it, but sat down quietly, happy at least that there was no stupid chattering out here. The tree stood silent, and there was no conversation between them, as there once had been. "I planted you," he did say reproachfully after a long time, but if it stirred at all in answer, it was far too near the top for him to see.

It was getting very dark, and he ought to go back to the stuffy kitchen, where he would have to parry endless questions about where he had been. Before he went, he would say one spell, the first and simplest he had uttered, when long ago the spirit of the tree had revealed itself by slaying the overseer who threatened it. He crawled back into his lair and fumbled in the loose earth about him for his offerings of pretty stones. Then he turned himself onto his back and said the words, looking straight up into the darkness of the branches. After a moment, with the tiniest of sighs, the tree began to answer him.

It answered with a whisper, a stirring, a lashing, a rumble, a flash, and a roar. It whipped and bent to the storm as the heavens were opened and the water streamed down, as if from the overflowing of some heavenly Nile. Roofs were blown off in the slave quarters and mud walls melted down to shapeless lumps. Pools of water extinguished the fires all over the kitchen. In Pharaoh's quarters, the god's own bed was hastily moved from under a drip. People huddled together in the torrents, shivering and wailing, while the children shrieked at the lightning flashes, and men spoke of the end of the world.

It was a terrible time, and yet it was quickly over. In the steaming damp of the following day, mud walls were rising again. Children were gathering palm leaves for roofing. Painters and workmen were busy repairing the damage to the solider parts of the house. On the second day, things were so nearly in order that the gardeners could take out their men to pick up torn branches and cut off battered flowers.

The tree by the rubbish pits had blown over. "That is a pity," said the chief gardener, "for this tree was one which Pharaoh placed himself. We must find another for this spot, but meanwhile, be sure you save the wood."

"There is an old man here," exclaimed one of the slaves who was nearest. "The tree is lying across him, and I think he is dead."

"What an extraordinary thing!" said the chief gardener, peering through the branches. "Does anybody know who he is?" Nobody did. "Well, I suppose you two will have to bury him somewhere."

"By the by," said the head chef four or five days later, "what became of the old dodderer who used to sweep round here? Does anybody know where he has got to?" Nobody did.

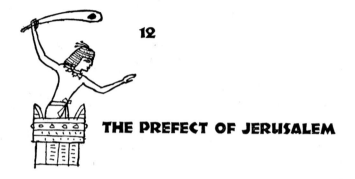

12

THE PREFECT OF JERUSALEM

THERE WAS a dark cloud coming eastward over the watershed, blackening out the dusty olive orchards on the terraced hills and whitening by contrast the arid limestone cliffs. For the first time in two months, it was going to rain. There would for a while be an end to sandstorms, to wearing a veil across the face, to sparing water. Mena sighed. Of all the delights of Egypt, the one he missed most through the years was abundant water. In Jerusalem, when the stinking cisterns had been drained of their last drop, the whole town was forced to rely on a single spring, whose supply must be rationed carefully. Hence, no doubt, the all-pervading dirt. In the brief, hot lull before the storm, the fetid smells were almost intolerable, even after twenty years and with the knowledge that a cooling wind would in a few moments blow the worst of them away.

For the thousandth time, Mena took a moment to regret the days when there had still been glamor in the military life. He had been the only son of quite ambitious parents who had intended him from his earliest years to be a scribe. If he had been less bold and active, or the schoolmaster less ferocious, he might have become so. Actually, he grew tired of savage beatings and ran away as he was entering his fifteenth year. Those were the glorious days when Pharaoh still rode before his regiments himself. Mena had liked the foraging parties, the cooking and sleeping in the open, the chance of getting wonderfully drunk in a good wine country, the marvel of seeing the sea, and the sense of belonging to a superior race amid jabbering Syrians. He had even enjoyed the excitement of battle, the inevitable victory, and the thrill of receiving his first gold ring for valor or of being made captain of his first company.

Those had been golden days. Mena's skill in writing had been discovered by his superiors, and it brought him rapid promotion. His daring had become notorious. It had been Mena who led the famous contingent that Tutiyi had smuggled into rebellious Joppa, concealed in enormous water jars. His reward had been an independent command with a chance, he was told, for fame and easy riches. Tutiyi had procured him the prefecture of this little hill town, Jerusalem.

Mena had often wondered whether Tutiyi could have been jealous and anxious to keep all the glory of the taking of Joppa to himself. Jerusalem, after all, was not even on the main route through Syria. All the traffic went up the coast from Gaza and passed her by. Not for Jerusalem were the Egyptian traders, the important ambassadors, or the detachments of troups going up to settle feuds among the cities of the north. All that ever came from Egypt was a yearly escort to fetch the tribute King Abishua exacted from his subjects and paid over, with suitable deductions, into Mena's treasury. With it Mena or Abishua himself would be privileged to send letters to Pharaoh, chiefly consisting of expressions of loyalty incised in blunt characters on tablets of

baked clay. At the end would come a request, long medi-
tated, but compressed into a sentence or two that concealed
aching months of alternate hope and despair. "Send me back
my grandson, Abdi-khita," wrote Abishua. "I grow old,
and is he not my heir?" "Does Abdi-khita still live?" There
was never any answer.

When Mena wrote, he had sometimes better fortune.
Lately he had been desperate for reinforcements to control
the shepherd tribes who were migrating from beyond
Jordan. The preceding caravan had brought him help. Out
of his infinite magnificence, Pharaoh had spared Jerusalem
five men.

If he could have wept on this occasion, Mena would have
done so; but all his tears were dried up by twenty years of
longing for home. Instead, he made the usual feast for the
captain of the party, pressed the usual bribe into his hand,
and tried as always to detain him for the sheer pleasure of
talking with an Egyptian again. "At least let Abishua send
you out an escort," said he. "The road is scarcely safe, and
you are leaving half your soldiers behind. We have been
training the people here, and truly their archers are not bad."

The captain, who was anxious to get back to more civi-
lized quarters in Gaza, accepted this offer, foreseeing that the
Syrians would be useful as donkey drivers to get his pack
animals over the hills. Of Syrian soldiery, he had no opinion
at all. To him indeed, these lonely hill-town prefects were
all the same. All of them were pathetically anxious to talk
Egyptian gossip and would brag about their own achieve-
ments as though they were generals, not broken-down old
soldiers, gone half native in the course of years. This fellow
in Jerusalem, for instance, was wrapped in a greasy woolen
Syrian robe.

The wind was rising now. In a few moments it would rain. Mena went over to his chest and took out the offending Syrian garment. He was a fastidious man, but a heavy robe was a necessity for much of the time in this climate. When the cisterns were full, there might be a chance to get it washed.

Abishua appeared on the threshold just as the rain started. Mena made him a courteous inclination. Part of his work was to uphold the dignity of Abishua as king, in spite of the tremulous indecision that had grown upon the old man since his repeated requests for Abdi-khita had been made in vain. Abishua had not himself been brought up in Egypt, but for a year or two he had been a hostage in Memphis and golden

On. Since then, he had been consecrated king with Egyptian holy oil, would sacrifice occasionally with Mena in Amon's little temple, and paid over the tribute with only a reasonable amount of grumbling. In fact, he had been a model king, not too ambitious to be ashamed of owing his throne to Mena's dozen soldiers and to a widespread fear of Egypt's sleeping power. Latterly he had begun to doubt whether the name of Abishua counted for much in Egypt, and to wonder whether Bela, his nephew, would not suit Pharaoh just as well, especially if Abdi-khita should happen to be dead.

"My lord the king does his poor gatehouse honor," said Mena bowing low, not out of respect, but for the benefit of watchers. Jerusalem, perched behind rough stone walls on a narrow ridge, was intensely crowded, so that even the king found it hard to command an instant's privacy.

With a fierce crash the storm broke, drowning Abishua's reply in pouring rain. In the half-light, Mena could see that he gestured, shook his hands above his head as though in frenzy, and then smote wildly on the ground before him with his staff. Mena was used to such scenes, which were growing all too frequent as the old man sought to lay the blame for his feebleness elsewhere. Despising such effusions, he yet forced himself to step within earshot and was rewarded by having something square and heavy thrust into his hands. "Look at it," screamed the old man. "Read it. Abdi-khita is surely dead, and no one any longer cares about our fate!" He put up his hand to his beard and tore at it ineffectually as though, had he the power, he would have dragged pieces of it out by the roots.

Recognizing by feel the little baked clay tablets, Mena spared a moment to wonder incredulously if a messenger had found some secret way over the wall. As captain of the gate, he knew perfectly well that no stranger had entered Jerusalem for several days. He had himself sent out a party to scour the hills in case the road had been blocked to travelers by some robber foray. These thoughts passed through his mind as he took the tablets to the window and began to study the stubby little characters that had been punched on them while the clay was wet. He could not himself read well in this language, yet surely there was something familiar in these opening lines. "My father, lord of the lands," they said, "my god, the breath of my life . . . I prostrate myself seven times before my king, I, Mena, the dust beneath his feet."

There was much more, but Mena did not read it. Well he knew the flowery list of compliments, and at the end the desperate sentence beginning, "The lands of my lord and Pharaoh are perishing." Night after night he had brooded over this message, altering a word here or there, imagining its reception, saying to himself, "Surely someone about Pharaoh will remember Mena and know that he does not give way to imaginary fears."

Mena looked at his letter to Pharaoh which he himself had entrusted to the scrawny captain, adding a handsome bribe out of his own gold. He said nothing. He only swayed a little with the dizziness of extreme rage as he thought of his hands about the neck of that captain. After a moment, he mastered himself and said to Abishua a little hoarsely, "How comes my letter here?"

"Thrown out on the roadway!" screamed Abishua. "Tossed away by that dog of a captain like so much dirt. Pharaoh has given us up, or he would not have dared."

"Never believe it!" declared Mena, forcing his voice to sound quite confident. "Has not the good god sent us men?"

"Five men!" said Abishua scornfully, "and you were but eleven. I must let Bela open our wells to the shepherd people and take their chieftain's daughter into his harem. Without a troop of soldiers, I can hold out no more."

It was indeed true that trade was dying because the roads were no longer safe for unescorted travelers. The olive orchards on the hills around could now only be cultivated if Abishua posted scouts. Though open war was not yet waged, men disappeared and outlying farms were mysteriously harried. A party in Jerusalem even desired to abandon the hills to the wild shepherd folk and to make the best of the situation by a treaty. Leader of these was the king's nephew, Bela, who had been heard to say that as long as the Egyptian tribute pressed heavy on the people, they had not the resources to combat the shepherd chiefs. It was known that Bela had asked for a shepherd chieftain's daughter, and that messengers had been back and forth, settling terms. It was even natural to suppose that the lives of Abishua and the Egyptian garrison had been discussed.

All this was fresh enough in Mena's mind as he argued with Abishua, trying to infuse into the old man a little of the royal dignity which alone stood between them all and death.

"Let me at least send on this letter to Gaza," he pleaded, "before anyone knows that the captain failed to carry it."

"They all know!" cried Abishua, wringing his hands. "It was Bela's man who found the tablet, and the whole city is buzzing with the news that Egypt has forsaken us."

There would be revolution over this, thought Mena. The end was indeed at hand. Bela's publication of such a story was in itself a proof that he meant to take advantage of Egypt's negligence. This very night, his assassins might dispatch Abishua. Tomorrow or the next day, the gatehouse could be stormed and an alliance patched up with the robbers in the hills. Unfortunate that Mena's own patrol had not picked up this letter, but these things happened. Meantime, at least it rained.

"Thothmes!" Mena stepped quickly between Abishua and the doorway, raising his voice to summon his young lieutenant from the outer room. "How full are the cisterns now?"

"Not very full, my captain, but there is drinking water for ten days."

"It is good. Take King Abishua and shut him up in the

tower. Put one of the men on guard there, and come back to me."

In an hour the sun would set, and after that it would be some time before the palace servants missed their king. They would suppose Abishua was lingering after a scene with the captain, which he often did in order to bolster his failing courage with wine. There should still be a few hours of the old king's reign in which a cautious man might make some moves.

Young Thothmes came back and stood before him. Mena regarded him thoughtfully. He had been brought up in the garrison, was in fact the son of a soldier by one of the native women, though by chance he happened to look like a pure-bred Egyptian. This had recommended him to Mena, who had in a casual way adopted him, needing perhaps some reminder of himself when he was young. He thought of himself now, crammed into a jar and bumped and jolted on a donkey's back into Joppa. It had been his glorious hour, and he could only envy Thothmes, whose adventures lay ahead.

"I am sending you to Gaza over the hills," he began abruptly. "It will take two nights if you travel in secret and keep off the trodden paths. Carry water, and avoid the wells where you may be discovered. Hide during the day. We must have help from the prefect of Gaza, whether he is willing or no."

Thothmes nodded as though he too had come to this conclusion. "If I leave by the gate, I shall be seen and followed. I will go out through the watercourse," said he.

Mena carefully thought this over. It would be a secret way out of the city, but by no means an easy one. There

was but one spring in all Jerusalem which never failed, and
this naturally lay in the valley, in a cave below the walls.
To it a sloping tunnel and a deep shaft had been cut right
through the hillside, in order that the people might still
draw water if the town were besieged. To climb down that
forty-foot shaft was not impossible, yet dangerous in the
dark, with rocks below and with the rope that drew the water
rotting, as it always was, from age and use. "You will be
dashed to pieces in the shaft," said he.

Thothmes shrugged his shoulders. "I must take my
chance," he answered. "Certainly there will be watchers
on the walls, and if I am seen going out by the gate, we shall
be all undone."

This seemed so likely that Mena made no more objections,
though if he could have spared another messenger, he would
have sent a second man out over the wall. Since this was
impossible with a garrison of ten, he dismissed the matter
from his thoughts and began to consider what was now best
to be done.

The gatehouse at Jerusalem consisted of two square
towers, each originally a rough stone structure with a flat
roof and parapet above. To this Mena had added a second
story built of wood and excellently loopholed, again finished
off with a flat roof and battlements. Each tower was itself
a strong point, but together they were not particularly well
adapted for a siege. They had been designed, of course, to
protect the gate and not to house the garrison, which lived
in outbuildings along the inside of the wall. Mena's tower
contained the armory; the other, the bulk of the stores.
Both had small supplies of water, neither adequate. It had
become urgently necessary to consolidate these things.

What decided Mena in favor of his own tower was the

superior strength of his door, which was of heavy wood
and closed upon a pivot set into the stone. This should
resist some battering, especially if it were reinforced from
inside. Fortunately, the roof was well supplied with ammunition in the form of great piles of heavy stones. More
would be obtainable from the other tower if there was time
after bringing over stores.

It was a dim night luckily. The moon was covered, and
the steaming of the hot earth had produced a little mist. To

this and to Abishua's disappearance, Mena attributed the delay that allowed them to continue their work for several
hours. When at last the sentry on the roof reported cautious
movement in one of the alleys across the little square, Mena
gave instant word to the men detailed for that duty to desert
the second tower after setting it on fire. If he could not
hold it himself, he could at least deny it to Bela, and by doing
so he could maintain his own possession of the gate.

There was a tense silence after this for about half an hour, since the fire gained ground slowly, and in the darkness the watchers from the alley did not at first perceive the smoke. Indeed, Mena supposed that the first movements had been those of a party detailed to slit the throats of himself and his men while they were asleep. Discovering that their victims were astir, they had most likely gone back to Bela for instructions, thus missing their chance to seize the abandoned tower before too late. At all events, it was not until red began to glow through the loopholes that a yell rent the darkness as somebody perceived what had been done. This was answered by other shouts farther back in the town, and followed by screams and barking. In the midst of the noise, a confused rush was made by about a dozen men to save the tower. Mena's bowmen let fly from the roof and even in the darkness claimed three victims, one of whom let out such a fearful shriek that his companions stopped in their tracks. Most of them now retreated hastily to the shelter of the lanes across the square. Three or four reached the tower and, finding the door closed, ducked behind the building, out of sight. Even if they dared come round to the entrance, however, it was now apparent that the fire could not be put out by bare hands. Great columns of smoke were rising and a flame burst out of one of the loopholes, illuminating the scene with a reddish glare.

The whole town was evidently waking in confusion. Having gone peacefully to sleep as Abishua's subjects, the people were aroused in the darkness to find fire, uproar, corpses, the rule of Bela, and the overthrow of Egypt's power. Long debated as the thing had been, its coming was so violent that men who might have stood aside now seized their weapons, dreading massacre. The clash of arms, the screams of frightened women, and the shouts of cornered men rose wildly through the town.

It was this tumult that saved Mena's garrison. The night was still, and they had not waited for the dawn breeze before they fired the tower. Now as the flames licked across the gateway, Mena was forced to put all his men on the battlements with sticks, hides, and as a last resort the precious water, praying silently for the coming of a wind. Blinded and choking, they leaned out into the smoke with soaked hides, beating frantically at the hot, charred surface of their own battlements. Once the wood burst into flame, water enough to keep a man alive for fourteen days was poured on it. When at last they could rest, put oil on their blistered arms, and watch the dawn wind blowing away the smoke from the blackened ruin, a hasty calculation showed that most of the water in the fort had been consumed.

"It may rain," said Mena nonchalantly, "and in any case, there will be help from Gaza." He spared a thought for Thothmes, wondering if the young man's broken body lay uselessly in the darkness at the foot of the water shaft. Such guesswork being quite unprofitable, he preferred to consider the position caused by his mastery of the Jerusalem gate.

There was another, lesser gate to the city which would of course be open to the people, and in any case the entire wall could not have been controlled by so few. On the other hand, the town could not be closed to Egypt as long as Mena remained the master of this entryway. Bela's people would not find it easy to assault him, now that the tower which would have commanded his own had been destroyed. They might prefer a blockade, guessing at the shortage of water and being assured that the city was cut off from in-

quisitive travelers by the shepherd men. One assault at
least was probable, but Bela would very likely delay it until
dark. By that time the tumult in the town would certainly
be over, ladders could have been collected, and a battering
ram brought up to smash the door. Mena decided to take
his men off the roof, as heat would make them thirsty, and
it was wise for them to sleep whenever they could.

It was hard to rest that day because of the noise. The
square by the gateway, like all open spaces in Jerusalem,
was tiny, and many of the garrison had women and children in the town. Fortunately most of these men were out
on patrol, presumably lost, while the five new soldiers were
unmoved by the frantic pleas of people whom they could
not help. However, these were not to be prevented from
screaming at the garrison, or more truculent citizens from
adding insults and threats. After the first hour, Mena forbade his soldiers to dry up their throats by shouting answers.

In this emergency, it was an unexpected help to find that
Abishua, so vacillating when danger threatened, could show
resolution when absolutely cornered. Bela's open rebellion
had made him no longer a hostage, but a rightful king fighting for his life. As such his position gave him authority,
and Mena could hand over affairs to him while he attempted
to snatch some sleep.

The assault came about midnight. The stars were out,
but the bowmen had only time to release a single volley
before the men with the ladders were across the tiny
square. The battering ram, being heavy, came more slowly.
The three archers Mena had ordered to deal with it had
shot five men before the rest dropped it in the doorway
and raced off, allowing the garrison to turn their whole attention to the ladders.

The men with these were more determined and far more numerous. Undoubtedly it was their hope to plant so many that Mena's little company could not dislodge them all. Once the weight of two or three men was on a ladder, a single man on the parapet could not easily knock it down. This reasoning was sound enough, but the tower was high, great stones lay ready, and half the fort was not assailable, since it lay outside the city wall. More than a dozen ladders were placed and dislodged. Others were planted, but the confusion of falling stones and writhing bodies made this difficult. One man alone reached the parapet, and him Mena slew with a spear thrust which went right through his body and bore him back with fearful force on the man behind him. He too toppled and, grasping at the ladder, brought the whole structure crashing to the ground. With wild shrieks the assailants broke and ran for cover, whence they contented themselves with shooting off their arrows at the roof. This being well protected, it could be but chance if any found a mark. Nevertheless, Mena withdrew his men into the tower and forbade his archers to use up precious ammunition in return.

It was pure bad luck that by some minor miracle an arrow should find its way in through a loophole and transfix Mena through the lower part of his left arm. To be sure, they stanched the blood after a time, while he told his soldiers that he was lucky to be no archer and that a spear needed nothing but a good right arm. Still, it was painful, and he was conscious that wounds would not heal as quickly now as they had done when he was young. He lay back on a cloak they had spread for him and tried to summon his resources. There was a short spell of silence, broken only by the groans of the men beneath the tower. With a savage look, the Nubian among his soldiers made a movement to get up and deal with them.

"Let them crawl off if they can," Mena ordered. "It is better than piling up dead men before our door." This was so indisputably true that no one protested, and presently the sounds in the square died painfully away.

Thus passed the second night, the one on which Thothmes might reach Gaza if he had survived the climb down the watercourse and the perils of the way. All depended on the prefect there, his troops, his readiness to push into wilderness country on the strength of a strange young man's report. There was no point in wondering about it except that his wound kept Mena wakeful. Either help would come, or it would not.

On the next day there was much hammering in the city, from which, and from the abusive threats of the people, it was evident that a different kind of attack would be prepared. The proper way to assault a tower was from high wheeled structures, consisting of a thick framework of timber covered with layers of hide. However, because Jerusalem streets were narrow, it was difficult to conceive of bringing a large enough engine through the town. Outside, the ground fell away too steeply for an attempt of this kind to be practicable. Mena was slightly puzzled, but as a precaution he had the men hoist their heaviest stones up on the parapet. Abishua directed this effort while he himself lay quietly, husbanding his strength, for his wound pained him. Thus passed a long, hot day.

The second assault came also by night, though as there was moonlight, the attackers had very little to gain from the protection of the dark. Unable to make his structures large enough to reach the parapet, Bela had determined to assail the wooden story of the tower. Accordingly, two smallish buildings came rumbling into the square, each one containing about ten men armed with axes and pushed from behind by twice as many more. The night was not too dark to see them clearly, but being powerless to stop their advance, Mena ordered his archers to let them alone. "Aim at those with ladders who will run in behind them," he advised. "When these towers are once in place, you may smash them down with stones. Meanwhile the Nubian and I will fight with the axmen through the loopholes, and when they are destroyed will come up here to your help."

Once more the hills resounded with the fierce yells of the laddermen who, advancing from behind their wheeled towers, flung themselves desperately upon the wall. Being, however, crowded by these two clumsy erections, they were unable for the most part to find room and jostled each other, or fell back into shelter to await their turn. Meanwhile, the huge stones crashing down from the parapet broke through one roof of hides and fell, amid hideous screams, on the group beneath. The other tower held firm, but rocked as though it would fall over, preventing the axmen within it from commencing their work. Quick as a flash, the Nubian stabbed with his spear through a loophole, claiming one victim before the fight could here be said to have begun, but in another instant his spear had been snapped off short, and axes were thudding heavily against the wooden wall.

Now Mena saw that he had disposed his forces badly, as the structure which was in action was exposed to only one loophole. Moreover, the men in it had a rough shield that they had raised on this quarter, thus keeping him and the Nubian idle when they might have been active on the

roof. The wall, though stout, was splintering. If the axmen smashed it, the garrison might not have the power to
defend the hole. Preoccupied now with the men upon the
ladders, Abishua and the soldiers could no longer have time
to deal with the wooden towers below.

There was no moment to be lost. Throwing aside his
spear, Mena darted for the steps and with the Nubian at
his heels burst out upon the roof. Without so much as a
glance at the struggle by the parapet, he made for the
brazier that he had caused to be lighted and set well back
in the farthest corner in readiness for just such a desperate
emergency. On it stood a small but furiously boiling pot
of oil. Snatching at his robe as he ran and using it to muffle
his hands, he seized the jar and, regarding neither the pain
of his wound nor the charring of the stuff beneath his
fingers, he ran clear across the rooftop and hurled it, pot
and all, at the roof of hides below.

A few hides, already battered heavily by stones, could
provide but little shelter from even a small amount of boiling oil. With screams of pain or terror, the axmen deserted
their post and ran for their lives, only anxious to escape
before the garrison threw more. Meanwhile the powerful
Nubian, flinging himself with a roar into the struggle by
the ladders, brought sufficient help to turn the scale.
Within five minutes the assault was completely abandoned,
all that remained being some groaning forms in the square
and the battered machines, on which the garrison were already throwing fire.

During this last repulse, Mena had lain huddled by the
wall in sick half-consciousness, fighting with the pain of
his scorched hands and wounded arm. As the Nubian came
to him with water, he roused himself to order the men to

bring out one of their two skins of wine. Abishua, he saw,
was also lying in a huddle, as were two of the archers and
a man he did not know. Evidently he was an enemy who
had succeeded in surmounting the wall.

"Throw that man over the parapet," he ordered brutally,
reflecting that he had no choice, since there was not a drop
of water to spare.

Two swarthy Amorites among his soldiers laid hold of
the victim, who struggled madly, shrieking to them to spare
his life. "Ask my father for ransom," screamed he. The
men took no notice, but Mena glanced at him sharply and
told the Amorites to stand aside.

This man was well known to all of them and might be
far more valuable alive than dead. He was one of Bela's
sons, a lad named Saul. To be sure, Bela had more than
twenty children, as was to be expected of a man with seven
wives. There was, however, a chance that Saul might be a

favorite and that negotiations might be spun out for some time. Mena's arm was throbbing with fever; his burned hands were almost helpless. One man lay dead, two more were wounded, and old Abishua seemed exhausted. It was clear that another attack would overwhelm them, and yet the people from Gaza might arrive if they held out till daylight came. "We will keep you," decided Mena, "but your father must send you water, for we have none to spare." Surely such an admission would convince Bela that the tower would fall into his hands after a very short blockade.

The next day passed in idling, sparing water, and vainly watching the road up which the help from Gaza must come. The weather was intensely hot and dry, and in this season might easily remain so over a week. There was a little wine, and a few spoonfuls of water were doled out at regular intervals to every man. The hours went very slowly as the garrison looked in vain for the rescuers, who should by now have come. Today the men were thirsty, but tomorrow they would be frantic. Meanwhile the prisoner, though in one sense a protection, represented temptation of a more subtle kind. Old Abishua spoke of this to Mena as the two were sitting together watching the road in the light of the setting sun.

The old man was in fact but slightly wounded, yet his face was ash-pale from exhaustion and sunken as though he were very near to death. He had sat in his chair during the day and had spoken cheerfully, but it was clear to all who looked on him that he would not fight again. He now glanced anxiously about and bent his head toward Mena, lowering his voice to a murmur the soldiers could not catch.

"There is no more water," said he, "and without it, the men will not endure another day."

"Gaza may yet send help," said Mena. "If not, it may rain."

"It will not rain tonight. Tomorrow the men will make some terms with Bela, who will spare their lives to save his son."

"They cannot suppose that Bela will keep such promises."

"Perhaps not," muttered the old man, "but any chance seems better than a death of thirst on this accursed tower. You and I must be killed, but these men are not pure Egyptians and might be spared to act as officers in Bela's guard. I think they sent out some message when Bela gave his son a little water, and that they will betray us in the morning if rescue has not come."

Once more a vision of the broken rope dangling in the water shaft rose before Mena's eyes, though he was far too old a soldier to be shaken by such thoughts. "Old friend," said he to Abishua, "you fight bravely to the end."

Abishua smiled with pleasure at the compliment. "It is easier to fight than to rule," he remarked.

Mena looked over his shoulder at his men sitting glumly together, and at the three wounded stretched on pallets along the wall. "There is still a little wine," said he aloud, "and as the sun goes down, we will finish it. Then those who still can fight may sleep, while I will watch for all."

No one wasted breath in answer or protested that a whole night's watch was too much for a wounded man. The wine that might have lasted till noon, had they been sparing, was now brought out and eagerly consumed. Even this, Mena noticed, did not make the group less sullen, though it did dispose them more rapidly to sleep. They made their way to the roof, where they might be ready for action, while the wounded men and the prisoner remained inside.

Mena also went up to the roof, concealing the effort that it had now become for him to mount that stair. His wound throbbed and was hot. His head was dizzy with loss of blood and flushed from wine. Without speech, the men lay down in their corners, while Mena half leaned, half sat in an embrasure, watching the moon rise over Jerusalem for what he felt sure would be the last night of his life. He found it hard to die obscure, exiled, forgotten, thrown away by his country like a sword that has served its turn. Worse yet was the thought that he would remain unburied, though religion taught that the soul must perish if the dead body were not preserved. However, why should his spirit care to haunt these blistering valleys and to sigh throughout eternity for Egyptian streams? He would be content if his life had but been happy. He envied Thothmes, who must have died on his great adventure, instead of surviving to eat his heart out through inglorious years.

The soldiers were quiet now. Mena drew his dagger and tested how well his bandaged hand would grip. Midnight murder was a strange last duty, yet, if Saul died, the men could have no hope of making terms. How they could hold out long, he did not understand. Still, help might by a miracle appear, or it might rain. Mena set a very cautious foot upon the stair.

There was a lamp alight in the tower, so that torches might be kindled quickly if sudden need arose. Mena could dimly see that the wounded men were quiet, the prisoner at the end lying still as any stone. Twelve slow steps would take him down the staircase, and three quick ones across the floor. One hand must fall across the prisoner's mouth and the other with the dagger cut his throat. The man lay face up, and he must strike at the throat. Mena fumbled with his left arm in his robe and hoped it would obey him. There must be no sound.

He stood at the bottom of the steps now, with but three paces before him. One of the wounded stirred and muttered, but the prisoner made no noise. Mena took his left arm out of the robe and held it ready, wincing a little as it moved. His burned right hand closed slowly on the dagger, while he swayed dizzily with pain. Three quick steps across the floor, and he threw himself upon the man.

Young Saul was dead already. Mena saw it as his arm descended, and he checked himself, rolling forward on the corpse. The eyes were open, but quite unseeing, though they glittered at the lamp. Mena put his dagger away and reached for the light, that he might examine him. When they had first laid hands on the prisoner, he had seemed lively. No one had spared time since to look at his wound. He was a young man and vigorous, but he had died uncomplaining. He had made a good end.

Mena was turning away when he hesitated a moment. On an arm half concealed by Saul's robe, he had caught sight of a golden gleam. Riches could do nothing for Mena any more, but long habit bade him turn aside the garment and take a glance. He stiffened in amazement. The bracelet Saul was wearing was his own. That very ornament which he had received for valor and had bestowed on the scrawny captain in his great need came back to him on the arm of Bela's son. It was conceivable that the captain should cast Mena's letter into the ditch like so much dirt. It was not possible that he would have given a Syrian lad such an ornament of gold. Mena thought of the Syrian soldiers who had escorted the captain not so many days ago, and who were now with Bela. They might have killed the captain

and taken the tribute. They might have used it to buy
alliance with the shepherds. They might have brought the
letter back to arouse the town.

Mena saw it all, and he saw one other thing clearly. If
the tribute were delayed, a force from Gaza would come.
Indeed, it must have come already, had not the Gaza prefect
needed to collect sufficient troops to fight his way through
the hills. In vain was the errand of Thothmes. Help would
arrive if Bela were fool enough to wait for it, and if there
were rain. Time and water would save him. If Bela were
expecting a secret surrender, he might be willing to haggle,
even to ransom his son with water, provided it were not
enough to last a second day. Mena thought he would waken
the Nubian and persuade him first to try this plan.

It was indeed not till noon that Bela gave them water,
and little enough for men who had spent a hot morning
shouting over terms. They consumed it all before they
lowered his dead son down to Bela, for as Mena said, "When
he sees he has been cheated, he will assault."

The dead man was received with screams of fury and
showers of arrows, which came rattling about the parapet,
but did no one any harm. There was no mad rush across
the square, as Mena had expected. Instead, there was much
hammering, and smoke arose throughout the town. "They
are making sure of us," said Mena to the king. "This time
they will attack with pitch and fire."

Abishua made no answer to that, but looked at the heavens.
"I think that it will rain tonight," said he.

Mena smiled. "Old friend, you and I will never see that
rain." Nevertheless, his mind was already busy with a
scheme to cause delay. If the storm would but come early,

it might be possible that Bela would wait until the tower was dry again.

"How many trumpets have we?" said he to the Nubian.

"Three, my captain."

"Do you and the two Amorites take them and stand by the outer wall. When Bela's signal for attack is given, lift them up and blow them hard. Blow for your lives, and let the echoes answer as if the men from Gaza were to be heard behind the hill. Bela may delay to see why his scouts have not yet warned him, and he will consider what he had best do to save the town. If half an hour is lost in such confusion, it may yet rain." He spoke with boldness, yet he did not think that the storm could come in time.

"They are attacking," called a watcher by the battlements. "I can see their engines rumbling forward through the town."

"Blow then!" said Mena. He stood up and gripped his dagger, for no other weapon was light enough to be held in his damaged hand. "Lift up the trumpets and blow!" He glanced at the hills and reckoned yet an hour before the storm.

The soldiers blew, and the distant hills re-echoed. They waited as though listening, and blew again.

"They have halted," cried the sentry. "There is confusion in the town."

"Shout!"

They shouted and the trumpeters blew once more.

"That was no echo," cried the younger Amorite. "That was a trumpet!"

"Blow again!"

They blew, and amid the echoes rolling back, there certainly appeared to be a sound. If aid were near, it was not near enough, thought Mena. It would arrive with the storm. Nevertheless, he repeated, "Blow once more!"

Over the hillside, a man came running, shouting. He waved his arms to those who watched in the valley lest Mena and his men escape that way. He pointed furiously at the road behind him, and forward at the town.

"Help will come with the storm," said Mena, "but its report comes now, and that may save us. What use to fire the tower and lose the town?" They watched two men cutting up across the hillside, making a long detour to the second gate. The engines moving out of the alleys had stopped, and the crowd had melted. Torches had been thrown down and trampled underfoot. In the valley the scout had already reached the watchers. They crowded round him and were seen gesturing, until with one consent they too began to run toward the town.

"The Gaza men are in strength, it seems," said Mena. "Bela would be wise to save himself by flight into the hills." He walked across and sat down by Abishua, leaning his head against the wall and closing his eyes. "I have not slept since all this started," he said, "but it will be over now."

"It is over for us," said old Abishua in a whisper. "You and I will never rule or fight again."

"They must send you Abdi-khita now," said Mena. "They cannot let the power go to one of Bela's men. As for me, old friend, I shall revisit Egypt and see water running through the green fields once again." His head jerked forward on his breast, and he lifted it, peering. "I will leave you Thothmes," he added, "if by chance he is not dead. He was born in this town and will serve you and Egypt without ever aspiring to be other than he is."

The Nubian blew again. Mena slipped gently sideways and drifted off into an unconsciousness filled with murmuring streams.